Return to Paradise

by

Gay Miller

ACKNOWLEDGMENTS

I would like to acknowledge the roles the following played in the development of this story line, either through study of, discipline by, or association with them.

The Bible. My late mother, Violet and my sister, Gail, extant.

FACT:

Revelation 11:18   "And the nations were angry, and thy wrath is come, and the time of the dead, that they should be judged, and that thou shouldest give reward unto thy servants the prophets, and to the saints, and them that fear thy name, small and great: and **shouldest destroy them which destroy the earth."** *King James Version of the Bible*

PROLOGUE

Abigail was a life coach. It was her job to welcome back the dead to paradise. She had been three years old when the great climactic battle of Armageddon took place. Always represented as total destruction by a nuclear holocaust, the entire world became confused and disoriented when things began to happen with unseen hands instead of a nuclear bomb. Expecting wars between nations, soldiers were unprepared for the prophesied battle to be between they and their best friends, family and neighbors. Suppressed mankind stood still with amazement as things heated up to a crescendo of chaos that angered most of mankind, with the exception of those mild of spirit. Death and destruction were everywhere. No one was immune to the sights, smells and sounds of this battle. Some were affected more than others. Abigail's family were some of those who survived. She would grow up in a world that never again would see the destructive kind of pollution that existed prior to the great tribulation, which took place before the war. Since 1914, man had been destroying the environment and his own health due to greed and selfishness. Many people thought they had everything figured out but were totally taken by surprise at the suddenness of the blow that shut down systems and worlds. The initial attack by the governments against religion seemed a good thing at first but as time went by, the unrest and total disregard for authority gave way to a militaristic regime in most countries. It was the same all over the globe. Apparently, this was not met with approval of the Sovereign Lord and he stepped in.

Abigail and her family would spend the next one hundred years cleaning up and rebuilding civilization. They had eternity before them and the promise of a resurrection of dead loved ones to look forward to welcoming back to the earth. It was all there, in the Bible. No one would ever die again. As Abigail's family embarks on a new journey towards a brighter future, they are joined by other relatives, friends and acquaintances who rejoice in their new found benefits. To have peaceful relations with even the vicious animals was just one benefit. The restoration of the full use of their brain's power opened up a fantastic world of possibilities never before believed possible. She had been named after a great aunt Gail, who was also a survivor. Many a night she would listen to stories by her about the promise that kept them all brave and all looking forward to the fulfillment of promises by God. A promise of a new world free from greed and corruption awaited Abigail along with the undying love of a man who would win her heart one day. And so the saga begins.

Return to Paradise

Chapter One

2116 A.D.

Claudia opened her brown eyes slowly against the brilliant glow of the sun beating down upon her where she lay. She could feel the warmth embracing her upturned face as she allowed her eyes the time needed to adjust to the light. As her lashes flickered, a cool hand slowly crept into hers as if to support what was happening to her. She felt instant comfort. She started to turn her head towards the vicinity of the owner of the hand when a soft feminine voice whispered softly into her ear that she was all right now. Confused, Claudia opened her eyes even further and saw the outlines of green leaves on trees. As her focus became more acute, she was able to become more aware of what was happening. The last thing she could remember was a car smashing into the driver's side of her own vehicle and severe pain. The pain was gone. The vehicle was nowhere in sight. Instead there was warm sunlight, beautiful trees above her and a sweet voice of comfort filling her mind and sight.

"Where am I? What is happening? Am I dead? Is this

heaven?" She couldn't stop asking questions.

"All will be explained shortly." Said the soft voice off to Claudia's left. Claudia turned her head to see who the owner of the voice was and her eyes met with soft blue eyes that revealed a truly kind heart and genuine love. How Claudia knew this was beyond her kin but knew it she did. The owner of the kind eyes and soft voice took her hand and gently pulled her up to a seated position.

"Hello there. I am Abigail, your new world coach. Welcome to Paradise on Earth. To answer your questions, no, you are not dead now. You were but are now resurrected. No, this is not heaven. If you look up you will see heaven but all are resurrected to earth as explained in Revelation. As to what is happening, you have paid for any sins prior to your death and now have a wonderful hope of living forever in a Paradise on Earth if you so choose. It is all up to you now but Satan has been locked up for a thousand years and will not be influencing anyone for a long time. Take your time to view your surroundings. We don't usually receive resurrected ones out of doors so you must have loved the outdoors in your time on earth previously."

"I…oh yes, I did. I was a biologist. Was. Whoa! I mean "am" a biologist. I love my plants, flora more so than fauna. But I love animals, too. Now I am rambling. This is a lot to take in, you know."

" Yes, I know and you are doing quite well. Can you stand as yet?" Abigail asked, smiling.

"I think so. Yes, I believe I can even walk a little bit."

"Good. Let me show you the part of Paradise on Earth where you will reside for a start. It is in the area where the place was previously known as Florida. It has no name now except southeast region. There is no division between states nor countries as all borders have melted with the great battle."

"Great battle? What is that?"

"Well, did you ever hear of Armageddon?"

"Sure. Are you saying someone dropped a bomb and wiped everyone out?" Claudia exclaimed.

"No, indeed not. Armageddon was God's war, not man's war. Jehovah God stepped in before it was too late and decided to destroy all those who were destroying the earth. Oh, look over there! I imagine you have never seen that flower so big, have you?" Abigail pointed at Bougainvillea that's blossoms were at least four inches across. She went to pick a blossom.

"Look out!" cried Claudia. "There are huge thorns on that plant."

"Not any more. Thorns are a thing of the past. When protection was needed, they were there but that is not the case in

Paradise on Earth. All are safe here and thorns are not necessary. You will see many changes here now. I hope you will enjoy learning many new things as a biologist here."

Abigail levitated up to the level on the vine where the largest blossom grew. Claudia's jaw dropped. Abigail smiled and simply told her all would be revealed soon. She handed the flower to her.

"This will look lovely in your auburn hair."

"No, you are mistaken, my hair is gray now. It used to be auburn." stated Claudia matter-of-factually. Abigail just smiled and let it go. If she had a mirror with her, she would have shown her how her hair was already beginning to grow back to its original color with its luster, too. She must make a note to keep a small hand mirror in her pocket along with bird seed.

Claudia looked around in amazement as she spotted so many beautiful and diverse plants and trees. Then to her amazement even further, a beautiful multicolored parrot flew up and landed on Abigail's shoulder. Abigail chuckled and took out some seed from her pocket.

"The many birds here know me too well. Can't keep a secret stash of seeds anymore, I guess. Do you think you will like living here, Claudia?"

"Well, how could I not? What is the catch? What do I have

to do to be able to stay? If I don't pass the test will I end up in hell?" she queried.

"What!?? No, no no. You are so silly. There is no hell. Well, not like you've been taught. All there is is death, from which there is no resurrection. That will all be explained to you but I don't think you will have any problem meeting the requirements. All you have to do learn about our Creator and love Him and your neighbor. That isn't too much to ask, is it?"

Claudia thought for a minute and simply shook her head. If that was all it took, Claudia was ready to show the world what a loving person she could be. She couldn't wait to learn more.

"So, what do I do now?" She asked.

"What we will do soon is bring you to our next meeting and introduce you to the congregation. The elders will review your case and assign a sister to instruct you in the way. That is only for the purpose of making things clear to you. Things like the history of the world, explanations of what took place during the Great Tribulation, the battle of Armageddon and the history of Jesus. It is all there to enjoy and there is no passing grade, just learning fun. That is later, however, so for now I think we should get you settled into your home, which was designed and made especially for you. I am still amazed at how this all works."

"How what works?" asked Claudia.

"How the workers know what type home to build for you. They learn about you about three months before your resurrection and they build it to suit you. I am anxious to see your reaction to your new home. It is just around the corner, right on the beach."

"On the beach? Oh, wow! I love the beach!" Cried Claudia with excitement.

They walked a little further on and Abigail parted the large leafed plants to show a pathway. The sand sparkled as the sunlight glanced off its raised areas of the path. The warmth from the sun's heat filled Claudia's soul as the sand shifted between her toes. She hadn't noticed the lack of shoes before, just knew of the white shift of a dress clinging to her slightly rotund body. She frowned when she looked down and started to ask a question. Abigail anticipated her question.

"You were resurrected as you were when you died. Your body will begin to grow young again and will slim down with all the good food we now eat. Imagine a world with no preservatives. Can't wait, I bet, huh? You should already have noticed the lack of arthritis, though. Is this true?"

"Why, yes, now that you mention it. You know, this is getting better all the time. It is like a dream come true."

"I know what you mean. You know all those fairy tales where we are a princess waiting for our Prince to come? Well, our

Prince was Jesus and he is the one who is making our dreams come true. And now, here is part of your dream come true. How do you like your new home?"

Claudia turned from Abigail to view a grove of palm trees wherein set a large, thatched house with a twenty-foot verandah encircling the entire house. It was strange that it should feel like home so quickly but it did and Claudia was anxious to see the whole place. She walked onto the verandah and noticed that furniture and not walls divided the space. There was the space for a living room here and a kitchen area was over there with a dining alcove attached. It all wrapped the home. She ventured inside the lone room which itself was twenty feet squared. It was a sleeping area with closet. Windows were situated high to let in light but kept her privacy and the open feel of such a large room gave her a sense of warmth and comfort. She wandered over to her closet and noticed several more shift dresses hanging there along with some sandals. She turned a questioning eye to Abigail and Abigail nodded. Claudia took the sandals out and slipped them on her feet. Very comfortable, she thought. Smiling to herself, she strolled along the verandah to encircle it to see all that was now hers. When she got towards the back, she noticed another building that was totally enclosed but had an adjacent greenhouse attached. She whirled around to face Abigail.

"Is that what I think it is?" she asked excitedly.

"I guess so. What do you think it is?" Abigail smiled.

"A green house and a lab?"

"Then it must be so. To start your life here as normally as you had before, all efforts have been made to give you what you had. You must understand that you have an eternity before you and you will no doubt decide to venture forth into other interests as time goes by. However, this will give you some familiar surroundings to make you feel comfortable and help you get settled." Abigail now took Claudia's arm and guided her away from the property and more towards the ocean. When they got close to the shore, Abigail pointed to the sky.

"Look up at the sky now that we are out from the cover of trees." Said Abigail. "What do you see?"

"Well, I see the sun is up but I don't see any clouds much. And the sky is blue but it looks different somehow. What am I seeing, Abigail?"

"What you are seeing is the canopy that was over the earth when it was first created. That was how Jehovah had planned it initially and it is the best way for it to be in order for the entire earth to be productive. We still have seasons but they are balanced and not extreme as before. If you will recall our history, the flood of Noah's day was the first time it ever rained. That rain came from the releasing of the canopy of water that was over the earth at that time. So, even though you have a green house beside your lab, you really won't need it much. The whole earth is now a green house."

Just then, two manned, young lions approached the two women. Claudia gasped and turned, as if to run. Abigail grabbed her arm and shook her head.

"Do not fear them, Claudia. This too was part of Jehovah's promise to us. The animals would no longer be fierce nor violent but would instead be friendly as in the original garden. Predator and prey no longer exists. All are in subjection to us. They are friendly now. Go ahead and pet them. They love it. Actually, they can get pretty demanding if you pet them too much. And don't be surprised if you have several types of animals asleep on your verandah when you awaken each morning. That is why you have a bedroom with a door on it. It will keep the monkeys out of your bed." She laughed with her last sentence.

Claudia was having such a difficult time taking all of this in. It was just too wonderful and too much information at once. Her head was swimming with information and excitement. She spotted a couple of beach chairs up close to the tree line in front of her home and decided it was time to rest. Abigail knew where her thoughts were taking her and followed closely but giving her some space for privacy. They both sat down and took some silent time to stare out at the ocean as the lions curled up at their feet. Claudia

13

had so much to take in and to think about. These were all new things different from what she had been taught all her life. It didn't make sense and yet at the same time it made perfect sense.

A single mom in a world sans religion had raised Claudia. Her friends had often spoken of their beliefs and she guessed she had adopted some of their ideas without actually attending any services. Boy, were they in for a surprise when they got resurrected. She suddenly sat upright and turned to Abigail at the thought of others being resurrected.

"Abigail, have any of my friends been resurrected as yet? I mean, when did all this go down and what of my mother?"

"Calm down, sweetie and I will try to answer all your questions. Some I won't be able to answer, as I won't have that data but some I can answer. As to when, well, it happened about five years after you died. I know two of your friends made it through the battle as they had made some changes in their lives to include Jehovah in it. They will be around later to welcome you. Others will not be here. I'm sorry to tell you that they refused to accept the truth about the Kingdom and chose to believe false doctrines. They did not investigate any part of the Bible but just lived blindly by the modern trends. The war games their children played on the computers became training grounds for violence and everyone turned on each other at the end, just as it was foretold they would. But, as you know, your mother passed away five years before your own death and she will be resurrected very, very soon so that is something wonderful for you to look forward to, isn't it?" Abigail asked.

"Yes, I guess it certainly is. I'm sad for my friends who didn't make it. Well, in a way I am sad but it seems to be all right, ya know? I know there is so much to look forward to that I don't think I will have time to dwell on what might have been."

"That is right and I know you will really look forward to helping us get a place ready for your mother, won't you? Tell me about her."

"Oh, she was awesome. She was a strong woman. She had a great business mind and ran her own café in the better part of Jacksonville. I guess that is all gone, Jacksonville, I mean. But, she raised me by herself when my Dad died in World War Two. Hey! That means that I will get to meet my father, too, right?"

"Yes you will. But do you know what? I think it is time for us to grab some lunch, don't you? There is going to be a noon meal over by our town center so lets stroll along so that you can meet some others and get to know your neighbors."

They stood and shooed the lions away from following them and started down a path that Abigail chose, which was previously unnoticed by Claudia until the last minute. But she did notice a young man walking with a gorilla. Pushing up large banana leaves

15

and fern branches, they made their way about one hundred yards to an opening on an inlet bay area where fifty or more people were gathering around tables set with the most aromatic foods Claudia ever smelled. There was smoked fish, steamed veggies, assorted fruits, shell fish and breads fresh from the oven. There was no sign of any other meat except seafood so Claudia figured eating the friendly animals was something one didn't do now. Her stomach began to growl. Abigail laughed and said that some things will never change.

Both women filled plates with their choices and moved to sit at a round table that could seat ten people. There were five other people sitting there already and Abigail greeted all by name. She then introduced Claudia to them all and each came to give her a hug. She felt warm tears welling up in her eyes and took a moment when no one was looking to wipe them away. The general chatter was lively with all sorts of information being poured her way for her to ponder over tonight in bed, she assumed. For right now, she was starving and the food was the best she had ever tasted. The fruit tasted like it always did, though more intense. The fish, which she had not cared for much in the past, was delicate and light with no fishy flavor so she guessed they would share that secret with her later. The company was good, the food was good, the weather was perfect and Claudia was the happiest she had ever been.

A thundering sound suddenly broke up the general chatter as it grew louder and louder. Everyone stopped to stare at each other and then grins broke out among them all. The talking grew excited and Claudia couldn't make out what anyone was saying. She didn't have to wait long to make heads or tails of it as three huge elephants came stomping into the area with two riders each upon them. They were couples so Claudia guessed they were married couples. Married couples who rode elephants. Elephants. Claudia shook her head. She turned to Abigail.

"I don't think I understand fully what is going on here. Can you explain the elephants and the lions, please?"

Abigail grinned. "Sure. When Armageddon was over, the angels opened the zoo doors and all the animals came out to live freely and reproduce at will. These are the results of years of freedom. You know, you were dead for nearly seventy-five years before your resurrection. A lot has taken place since then. How are you feeling now, by the way?"

"Fine, I guess. I'm feeling great, actually. I haven't felt any arthritis pain at all. Nor aching in my bones. Isn't that something?"

"Yes, it is. Here is some other good news. We have few mirrors around now days but if you happen upon one check out your reverse aging process. You were fifty five when you died and

17

at this minute in your life, you don't look a day over forty, so that is something for you to look forward too, also."

Putting her hands to her face, Claudia turned to Abigail and grinned a huge grin. Then she removed her hands from her face to look at them. They already looked younger than she remembered. She liked this new world more and more with each passing minute. Looking up, she noticed that the crowd had dissipated. There was a couple sitting at the other table but they didn't look like they were ready to move on as yet. This would give her a chance to get to know some new people here. She motioned to Abigail that she was going over to greet them and with her nod of approval, she headed their way. Their backs were to her and they didn't see her approach. As she came around the table, however, she sensed a familiarity about them. They sort of looked like they could be the children of her old friends, Trent and Sandy. As she drew closer, they looked up and grinned with recognition. That is when she realized that this young couple was not their children but they, themselves. Her mouth dropped into and O and they both excitedly jumped up to run and embrace her.

They all started talking at once and many stories got started, ending with laughter and then hugs. Abigail watched for a few minutes more as she slowly realized that her job was now completed. She had introduced another person to the new world, to paradise. What a lovely way to start the day, she surmised.

18

There was nothing lovelier than starting someone out on their new life. Checking her pocket, she drew out a list she kept with her. She also withdrew a pencil and added a check mark next to Claudia's name. She looked at the next person on the list. Ah, Maxwell Winters. Sounds like a strong personality, she thought. Then she looked up to see a woman passing her with another new world coach. The woman looked vaguely familiar and when she turned to see Claudia running towards her mother, she knew. She smiled and waved good-bye to Claudia and turned to wipe away her own tears of joy before anyone saw them. She loved her job.

Chapter Two

2019 A.D.

Three years later

Gail looked around her new place in what used to be Florida. A small log cabin was all she needed right now and so it was built to her needs.

"Tell me the story again, Auntie Gail about how you survived.'" Begged the six year old Abigail, squirming on the stump by the fire glowing brightly in the oncoming darkness of the night. Gail knew this was coming and resigned herself to the retelling of her experience at the end of the old system. She sat down on the bench that was situated close to the stump in the front yard of her newly built log home. Sighing deeply, she began her tale.

"Well, just one more time, honey but lets make this the last time for awhile as we need to look forward, not back. Ready? It was 2016. The six women were all seated around the dining room table of the homeowner, Nathalie and if one were to listen in carefully, one could hear all six conversations they were each having over their cell phones.

"Well, I agree with you that God is amazing. As a matter of fact, in the Bible book of Psalms..."

"Would you like to know what it says about the last days of

this system found in the Bible book of...."

"Critical times hard to deal with...."

"The Bible promises to resurrect those sleeping in death as shown in John...."

"And in the days of those kings,...."

"I would love to stop by so we can discuss the Bible together..."

As a matter of fact, they were so intent and involved in their telephone conversations that they did not hear the sound of the military utility truck that pulled up in Nathalie's driveway. Nor did they realize that twelve military personnel, to include women, were piling out of the back end of the Army truck. As the group unloaded, half went around to the back of the house to find all exits in order to prevent anyone inside the house from leaving.

Inside the house, all six of the women stopped what they were doing when a pounding on the door startled them. Nathalie quickly ran to the window of her living room to check her driveway.

"It is the military with a truck to collect us, my sisters. Remember what we were advised at our meetings? Cooperate in any way, state your beliefs with conviction, do not bring reproach upon Jehovah's name. Well, are we ready for this? Let us have a quick prayer." They did so as the door resounded once again with stronger pounding than before. Nathalie quickly went to open the door at the prayer's conclusion.

21

"Can I help you gentlemen?" She said with a calmness she was far from feeling at the moment.

"Ma'am, as you know, Martial Law was put into effect two weeks ago. Under Martial Law, upon such approval, the department may use the authority of section 101(a) of the Act, 50 U.S.C. App. 2071(a), to control the general distribution of any material, including applicable services, in the civilian market. Therefore, Ma'am, I am hereby notifying you that this group of women who have been overheard making plans to distribute literature and services of Bible instructions with the possibility of a subversive nature to the general public is hereby under arrest. I recommend you do not resist this order in any way and cooperate fully under the command of the President of the United States of America. Do you understand this directive, Ma'am? If not, I will state it once again. Do you understand?"

Nathalie could only turn to the other women in the room and shrug her shoulders. The elders in the congregation had tried to prepare them all for such an eventuality but when it actually happened, it was more difficult to accept than she had ever imagined. There they were, just six divorced or widowed women who were trying to teach the Bible to any interested, surrounded by twelve people with weapons fully loaded. Cooperation seemed advisable at this juncture.

"It seems to be more appropriate that we cooperate with these people in the hopes that we will be able to make a defense soon. These ones are not in a position for us to negotiate with at all. They have orders and they must obey them. We have our orders and that is to cooperate until the day we will be awarded time in court for defense. Let us go, my sisters. Perhaps we will meet with others who can give us more insight."

They were escorted out to the trucks and assisted to climb into the back of the large, canvas covered, military truck. No one in the group of women was under the age of sixty and had to be given steps to climb into the back end of the truck. Once there, they were lined up along both sides with military personnel separating each of them from the other. Nathalie winked at Brenda and began to sing one of their songs; 'Ever onward, O my people, Let the Kingdom tidings go. Tremble not before our foe..'.

A male soldier at the front of the truck repositioned himself with abruptness and cocked his rifle. As the women under arrest gasped, he stated in no uncertain terms that all communication was strictly forbidden and that silence was recommended for the safety of all the prisoners present.

Nathalie decided that silence was probably their best option and just smiled at all her "sisters" with what she hoped was reassurance. Since there were no windows, her only choice of a view was out the back where the tarp was cinched, affording her their last glance at freedom. She bent her head to pray and with a slight peek at her "sisters", noticed they were doing the same. She prayed for wisdom, holy spirit, strength to endure, forgiveness and especially the hope that God's name would be sanctified.

Two hours later, they pulled into an area of tents that were completely enclosed by an eight foot high, chain linked fence with two feet of barbed wire rolls at the top of that. Their eyes widening at the resemblance to all the Nazi encampment videos they had ever seen and they turned to look at each other. They hugged themselves at the chill they each felt as the uncertainty of their future loomed ominously around them. The military personnel closest to the end jumped out and positioned the steps so that the elderly women could climb out and down the steps. Two men positioned themselves on either side of the steps in order to help but also to guard them from escaping.

All of a sudden, Frances walked up to one of the soldiers and started a conversation with him.

"Now, Benny, you mustn't be pointing that toy gun at the other children because you might scare them. What did your father tell you about that?" She rambled on.

The soldier she was talking to looked around nervously to see if he could find his Captain.

"Uh, Captain Belfort, sir! I think we have a situation, sir!" He looked around helplessly as Frances stood there picking imaginary lint off the soldier's uniform. His Captain approached with caution, all the while observing the actions of the elderly woman.

"What seems to be the problem, Private?"

"Sir, she seems to think I am some guy she calls "Benny", Sir!"

"I take it you are not the Benny she is referring to then?" He asked.

"Sir, no sir!" the soldier replied. The Captain chuckled at the private's distress and decided he would have to see that this elderly lady got to the medic and discharge his responsibility as quickly as he could. Before they had gone three feet, Frances squealed in delight and ran over to where some dandelions grew in profusion.

"I must pick some flowers for Momma! She loves yellow flowers. Benny, help me pick some flowers for Momma." She exclaimed as she bent over the weeds growing along the side of the old road that had led them to this particular encampment. The soldier looked at his captain with a queried look and the Captain laughed.

"Yes, Benny, pick some flowers for Momma." He threw his head back and laughed heartily at the look on the young soldiers face. In the meantime, Frances had picked a bunch of weeds and positioned them just under her eyes as if to smell them but instead she winked at Nathalie and then grinned as she turned to "Benny".

"Won't Momma be pleased?" she asked.

"Sure, sure. Now let's go show Momma." he stated and put his hand under her elbow to make sure she didn't take off running somewhere in search of "Momma".

The women had been gathered together that morning and had just finished their lunch by about fifteen minutes when they had started calling again. The disruption had brought the time up to one o'clock and now it was nearly five when they all saw "Benny" returning with Frances in tow. He stopped at the gate with his captive and motioned for a guard to open the gate. He gave her a slight nudge in, quickly shut the gate and turned to talk to his comrade in arms standing duty over that entrance.

"What was that all about?" the tall black soldier asked "Benny".

"I don't know for sure. I just know she was talking nutty when we left here but as soon as they fed her some orange juice and a cookie, she started acting normal again. So they had me bring her back here to lock her up."

"Hmm. Well that was interesting. Hope you had fun." he grinned and teased his friend.

"Ah, shut up!" Said "Benny" as he strode away to find something to eat himself.

Frances was greeted by the other five women and they surrounded her, asking questions and giving her hugs.

"What was that all about, Frances. You aren't diabetic, are you?" asked Katie.

"No, silly. I wasn't sure if it would work but I wanted to see how much I could find out through conversations within the offices if I could."

"Brilliant! But we will hear your information in a minute. First let me share with you what Brenda did. She was so clever, too! She went to the guard and asked permission to hang the clothes line that they had rigged up for us to use, a little higher. Yes! I couldn't believe my ears. She said "excuse me soldier but, would you mind if I climb this tower a little bit to put the line higher because we have big women that have larger clothes that hang lower to the ground when wet and I want to reposition the line higher to prevent that." He said sure, go ahead and so she climbed up the tower a little higher so she could look out over top of all the tents to see what she could see. And guess what? She saw that this is only one of about four encampments in a row here. She saw men in the next one. She couldn't see in the other two but we all became quiet to listen if we could hear anything and we heard a baby cry in the distance and then go silent like it was being tended to. What do you think and what did you find out for us?" Nathalie asked Frances.

"What you have spoken of confirms what I overheard in the medic's office. They are collecting all of we Witnesses and separating us according to groups so it wouldn't surprise me if we found many more encampments filled with teens, males, females, whatever. One of the things that I also found out was that they are not going to formally charge us with anything for as long as they can get away with it so that we won't be going before any judge or

27

court official anytime soon. They don't have to, under Martial Law, it seems. They say they are protecting the civilians from us. I am sure we will be told more as time goes by but I wouldn't count on it. The Constitution gets thrown out the window when Martial Law is declared, you know." Frances responded.

"So, sisters, come gather here so we can talk." Nathalie beckoned all over.

The women felt a mixture of anxiety, dread and euphoria all at the same time. They knew to expect this as it would mean the end would be fast approaching. For that, there was jubilation. But that didn't mean they wouldn't face trials and tribulation first. The immediate need seemed to be to take stock of their situation and inventory of anything they could find around the large shelter of a tent. The tent's walls had wooden framing as a house but the walls themselves were canvas of some sort. There were eight beds; bunks, if you will. Four of them lower and four upper. The youngest of the elderly women along with whomever was the smallest were delegated to the upper bunks. There were ladders at the end of each to help them climb to the top but it just wouldn't do to have this arrangement for long. They would have to make some sort of other arrangement. Why, one could break a leg if one fell from that height and had fragile bones as they.

They examined every square inch of the place, even checking to see if the previous tenants might have been Jehovah's Witnesses, also and left any literature behind. They found nothing on this turn around the tent but they would try again later. In the meantime, they decided it would be best to just sit on their bunks and wait for the next move.

It didn't take long for that to happen as two men came in to the fenced yard pushing a large cart with trays on them. Dinner! The women started to rush towards the cart as they realized how hungry they were but were told to halt immediately. They did so. Then they were instructed to approach one at a time to receive their rations. Obediently, the women did as they were told and were each given a meal consisting of some type of over cooked meat, mashed potatoes and peas with a roll. A single cookie lay on each tray, also. The women were completely grateful they had received anything at all and all took their trays back into the tent to sit.

"We will be back in one hour to collect the trays. If you don't give us your tray back, you will not receive your next meal." The soldier stated.

"Well, my goodness! What does he expect us to do with our trays?" Dolly asked. She was the oldest one at sixty seven years of age. Nathalie was the youngest at sixty, then came Brenda at sixty three, Katie at sixty four, Carlein was sixty five and a half and Frances was sixty six. All the women turned to look at Nathalie and she said that she would go ahead and give the prayer over their meal. Afterward, they took their trays to the sink to wash them. It was just a small bathroom type sink where they could wash themselves and anything else they needed. They were grateful for each convenience they found as they knew that could one day they could end up with absolutely nothing. Katie took the pile of stack-able trays to the gate and placed them just inside the gate. That way the guard would have to open the gate to retrieve them and if all the women were watching as he counted, they would be assured they would each get another meal. They were learning quickly how to take care of themselves.

Dolly, Frances, Katie and Carlein were given the lower bunks while the smaller, younger women, Nathalie and Brenda were allotted the upper bunks. There was room for two more women in this tent so they would possibly have to make adjustment for others should the need arise. They decided to check the tent out again before going to bed. They divided the space to explore, with all of them covering every area. They didn't want to miss anything. Everything they had on their person had been removed when they were searched prior to getting in the truck so they had nothing to start with. By the time they had all finished scanning over every inch of the property, they collected their treasures to inventory their finds. Frances was excited about something so they let her go first.

"Well, I didn't find this here but I did cop it from the doctor who examined me at the medic building." She revealed an ink pen. The women were thrilled with the find. With that they could communicate with others in the other tents or compounds. She also found a small bit of an emery board. She tossed her treasures in the center of the bunk. Nathalie had found three or four hairpins, some thread and a rubber band. Carlein found an empty envelope that was folded into a tiny square and placed under the leg of the bed to raise it up a little. Brenda also found a hairpin and an eraser from a mechanical pencil. An aluminum gum foil and a bit of clear, broken glass was also laid out from her pocket. The women began to grin at their store of goodies. Then they turned to Dolly, Katie and Frances for their finds. Dolly had found a button, a safety pin and a empty toilet paper roll. Katie was smiling as she pulled from her pocket a metal spoon that was bent nearly in half and wedged part way under the tent wall. She has almost missed it, she said but as her hand brushed some of the dirt off the floor, it had hit it and so she dug it up to bring to the pile. She also had found a penny. Frances was the last one to deposit her find into the pile and she hesitated a bit. Looking at each of the girls, she felt like she had failed them a little. She found only one thing, the last inch of an eye brow pencil. She shrugged and tossed it on the bed. Katie grabbed it and stated with delight that they could write scriptures on the tent wall with it. For encouragement. Frances' mood lightened up immediately and she suggested they all vote on which scripture should go up on the wall first. With that suggestion still in their minds, the sisters prayed after their long day and turned in to go to sleep.

The next day's activity came at daylight. The military guards changed duty and a breakfast of cold oatmeal showed up at the gate. Since the bowls were small, it took only a few minutes to finish it off as well as the two pieces of toast they each received. There was no sugar or cream added to the oatmeal but, as before, they were grateful they got anything.

A few hours went by in which they occupied themselves with exploring the exterior of the tent and the fenced area of their compound. There was a lot of space in the compound area and three more tents could easily fit in the area and still leave them with room for exercising. The women hesitated to go near the fence that divided their compound with the men's compound next to them. They were curious and yet apprehensive as to whether the men were "brothers" or criminal types.

"What are you doing Katie?" asked Dolly. Katie was kicking something with her foot and it was hard to figure out what it was.

"Shush. We don't want anyone to hear us. Come over here behind the tent away from prying eyes." With that, she gave the lump a swift kick that sent it bounding behind the tent where they were headed.

"Look at this! I made it in the wee hours before anyone else woke up. You know I can't sleep very well, especially in these conditions. Anyway, I got to thinking that we should try to communicate with the men in the tent next to us to see if they could shed some spiritual light on our situation or whatever information they have." Katie continued.

"Good idea. What does that have to do with this lump of mud?" Dolly asked her.

"It isn't just a lump of mud, silly. It is two pieces of dried mud that has a note in the middle. I made a mud ball last night and hid it under my bed so it would dry overnight. Then I took the broken glass to cut it in half. I used the spoon to scoop out a hole and put a note inside. Then I put the two halves back together and spit around the edges to "glue" it back together. I tied it with some of the thread, too." Katie grinned with her explanation.

"So, what are you planning to do with it? Oh, and what did you say in the note?"

"Well," Katie replied, "I said we were witnesses of a higher court and would they mind sharing their verdict with us."

"What! Oh, I get it. Code. You are nuts, you know that? I hope they understand what you are saying to them." Dolly grinned and then asked, "How are you getting it to them?"

"I plan to kick it over to the fence real nonchalant like and once it is on their side a tiny bit, just kick it for all its worth and hope it pops open on their side but out of sight of guards. What do you think of that?" she giggled.

"Like I said, I think you are nuts. But lets hope it works. What can I do to help?"

"Get the girls together and go to the opposite side of this area so that the guards will watch you instead of me. I will come to you all once I am finished."

33

"Gotcha. See ya soon." Dolly stated as she headed to where the other girls were standing around catching the sun's rays.

Katie waited until the girls were congregated on the other side of the compound and then checked to see what the guard was doing. He wasn't even bothered with looking at anyone. He just had his back to the compound and leaning against the small guard station. Katie then gently nudged the mud ball towards the fence between the two compounds. It rolled nicely. She pretended it was just an ordinary rock and put it in a zigzag motion as if playing a game. She wasn't sure if the men were brothers or not so she didn't want to draw their attention to her until she was ready. As she maneuvered the mud ball to the chain link fence, a final nudge sent it just under it but still within range of a good swift kick. Looking around, Katie saw no one was watching and proceeded to swing her foot back and let go with a wallop of a kick. The mud ball had been aimed at the back of the men's tent where a concrete post was positioned at a stay for the tents. It hit the post with a resounding thud and fell open to reveal a tiny piece of paper. Katie walked quickly away.

A man had just come out of the tent when the ball of mud hit the concrete post and he would have thought nothing of it if a tiny piece of paper had not started flapping as if to get his attention. He looked around to see if anyone was watching and no one was. A woman from the other compound was walking towards her companions so it was possible she had sent it over to them. He

34

used his foot to scuff it into the tent before he picked it up. Reading it, he began to smile. He understood the secret coded message and went to speak to the other brothers in the tent with him. Before long they were busy devising their own message to let the sisters know they understood and would reassure them somehow.

Since the guard station was positioned in the front of the tents, all those in the tents could have some privacy in the back yard area of the tents. This made it easy for the brothers to use their ingenuity to pantomime a reply to the sisters. They just had to wait for them all to return to the back of the tents. One brother had a crate that he turned on end so that it was like a table and he had placed a cup upon it. Five other brothers stood in waiting until the women started to come around to the back of their tent. When the first sister came around and happened to look up, she noticed a commotion among the men next to them. They frantically waved to her and Carlein put up her hand to stop them. Then she went to the other women to get them to join her behind their tent.

What they saw sent them into a fit of giggles, initially. Here were a group of men that were in the strangest positions they had ever seen. One man was next to a stand and a cup was upon it; the next man was standing at attention. The next two men were convoluted into a shape of some sort and then the next two were twisted with one sitting on the ground hugging the other man's leg. They realized suddenly it was a message and began to try to

35

unravel what was being stated. First they tried to figure out what the man with the coffee cup was supposed to be but it didn't seem to make sense so they went on to the next man. That didn't make sense either as he just stood as still as he could. The next two men were really strange as one was on the ground with his hand up in a curve and the other man was bent with his arm in a curve above the other man's. The final two men kept their original position with the one man hugging the others leg.

"Well for the life of me, I can't figure it out." stated Dolly.

"I can't either!" exclaimed Katie. The women scuttled about, whispering to each other except Brenda, who was just coming out the back tent door. She stopped to stare at the men. Then she burst out laughing. Everyone turned to look at her, including the men. The women came over to her to query her outburst.

"What are you laughing at, Brenda?" asked Nathalie.

"Those men. They are trying so hard to send us a message, aren't they?"

"Well that is what we figured. We are trying to decipher what it is, though." Said Carlein.

"Oh come on. You can't see what they are saying? It is as simple as the nose on your face. Maybe you guys were trying too hard or were to close to the situation." Laughed Brenda.

"Well, smarty pants, if you know so much then tell us what they are saying."

"They are saying to be of good courage." Explained Brenda.

"How do you figure that?" Asked Frances.

"Well, the first man looks like he is brewing coffee, right? Then the next man is straight and tall so he is probably the number one. The second two look like the number three. The big space is there before you get to the next two who look like the number six. He brews coffee...so Hebrews 13:6. It says "Be of good courage"."

All the women turned to look at the men in their shapes who were also nodding their heads vigorously. The women laughed and hugged each other and started to move towards the fence when one of the men, their brother, held up his hand to warn them against exposing their actions to the guard and the women backed away quickly. They had gained some headway in understanding their surroundings and didn't want to botch it by doing something so obviously stupid as give away their hand. But their smiles could not be hidden and their joy at finding brothers was evident to them only as they went about their day with more hope in their hearts than before.

They were still feeling elation later towards evening when a truck rolled up to their encampment and turned to back in to their gate area. Curiosity drew the reluctant women forward enough to view it but not enough to have the guards draw their guns to force them away from the gate. They had learned that lesson shortly after their arrival. Watching from a distance, they saw the back flaps swing open and four soldiers leap out on to the ground. One reached back inside the truck to withdraw a box which he put down on the ground to serve as a step. Then the same soldier reached up to pull the handle of the tailgate in order to open it up for the women who were sitting patiently for the next move. It was too dark inside to be able to see much except that they were women in dresses. The next thing to be removed from the truck was a folding cot, which was propped up against the fence beside the gate.

The first woman helped out of the truck was me." Gail continued her story. "The women inside the camp groaned their dismay that one of their sisters had been picked up and brought to the camp. They had been praying that no more sisters would be found. I was over seventy years of age and very gentle by nature. I was guided to the side away from the truck and escorted by a soldier who stayed by my side as if I would run away. The women inside the encampment waited on tenterhooks to see who else was coming out of the back of the truck. They didn't have to wait long as Joanne stuck her head out to see what was going on before moving down the step. It was quite a bit of a drop to the step and Joanne almost fell as she dropped down to the box. One of the soldiers literally grabbed her under her armpits and set her down beside me while I watched from the sidelines.

Both sides of the flaps were suddenly flung open as Linda

stood there with hands on hips staring out and around as if she were the one in control instead of vise-verse. The women inside the compound turned to each other and grinned. Then they sort of kept their mouths closed and waited to see what would happen.

"You there!" exclaimed Linda. "Come here and help an old woman down out of this contraption you men call a limousine."

The soldiers around her tried not to grin but a corner of the mouth turned up upon several of them. Two came over to help her climb out of the truck. She had not behaved at all on the ride over. They told her to be quiet and all she did was wink at them. They told her to stop singing and she hummed. They told her to stop humming and she whistled. They told her to stop whistling and she started drumming on the underside of her seat. This went on until they pulled up at the compound. She was tiresome, fun and annoying all at the same time. They felt sorry for the women they were going to leave her with this day. Little did they realize how much trouble she really wasn't. For Linda was terrified deep down inside and her distractions were for the purpose of praying as hard as she could.

After that, the men pulled away leaving the three of us and the cot just on the inside of the gate. They had other people to pick up and needed to get back to headquarters to get the list of other so-called dissidents. We were the easiest ones to pick up. We just came along nice and quiet like.

The three of us women stood stock still for a few minutes

39

until the truck turned the corner at the end of the dirt road leading to this compound. Then the other women already established there became very excited and rushed towards their three friends to envelope them in hugs and squeezes. The men next door looked on with delight that some more sisters were inside and safe. That was the situation as far as they could see it. The women were next door and safe. They weren't sure of any of the children, however. Nor were some of them sure about younger other women, such as their own wives. But all would be revealed soon, they felt sure.

Joanne was the first one of the newest arrivals to call for silence in order to share some news from the outside, which she knew all would be waiting for with anticipation. She began to speak when Dolly put up her hand to stop her. She then took her hand and escorted her to the back fence where they were closer to the men's area and they might be able to hear the report as well. Joanne understood and began to organize her thoughts in her head as they made their way to the back section of the encampment. Everyone settled down to hear. The men just lined up at the fence, unafraid of getting caught as they were too intent on hearing and could care less at this point. The rest of the women stood around in a semi-circle.

Joanne began; "Well, first of all, I am sure you all would like to know that all the minor children are with their mothers in a deserted Navy base area and are doing better than we here, apparently. They didn't want to risk children getting ill, I suppose.

That would raise some objections from the community. They are in a huge debate over what to do with us all, however. No one realized how many of us there were when they started this. Gail, Linda and I were detained in a police jail cell for two or three days and could overhear a lot of what the discussions were about regarding the Witnesses. Some still haven't figured out why we are being picked up at all. They don't realize it is part of Jehovah's plan. I hope." She finished.

The sisters turned to see the men slapping each other on the back with relief to know where their children and spouses were and that they were alright, for the most part. They turned to the women and gave them the thumbs up sign and moved away from the fence quickly so as not to give away the situation of communication they had with the women. Linda glanced up just in time to see one of the men and she recognized him right away. His name was unknown to her as he was with another congregation but she knew his wife was okay so she sent a shrill whistle out to him. He turned, as did others who heard the whistle. She gave him a thumbs up and a rapid nod of the head and his frown turned into a huge smile and a clasp of his hand to his heart. He was still grinning as he turned away.

Linda, on the other hand was dragged into the tent by two of the sisters with determination. They needed to apprize the three new occupants of the situation which would include Gail not whistling at the men, no matter what the reason. They didn't want

41

to lose any privileges they had acquired.

"My goodness, Linda, do you want to get us all thrown into a real prison or something?" exclaimed Carlein.

"What's wrong? What did I do?" asked Linda.

"You can't communicate with the brothers because they may move them or us and then we won't have even this much fellowship. Who knows, they may even move us to worse conditions then we have now."

"Oh, well, sorry. I didn't know. I will be more careful in the future. But are you sure? Because the men who brought us in seemed nice."

I started to laugh. "You have to forgive Linda. She is totally oblivious to what is going on around her at times. She didn't even realize when the men were being aggressive. They wanted her to be totally quiet and she just kept making noise throughout the whole trip."

"Maybe that was my plan, see? To push the envelope to see what we could get away with or something. Anyway, I will be extra careful in the future. I just thought you all might like to see something I brought with me, though."

That got the girls attention and they gathered in closer to see what was up. Linda grinned at them and then took out her dentures. There, wrapped in cellophane, was a white piece of paper. She replaced her dentures and then removed the wrapper to unfold a delicate piece of paper. It was a page ripped from the small print edition of the New World Translation of the Holy Scriptures. Revelation, chapter twenty one with parts of twenty and twenty two along with it. She tossed the cellophane in her shirt pocket and looked at each of her fellow sisters in the Truth to see their response. She was not disappointed at all. They were grinning from ear to ear and their excitement was manifested in their hugs with each other.

Then Joanne removed her dentures and another page came out. It was first Thessalonians chapters three and four with parts of two and five. Everyone looked at me and I just shrugged and said I didn't wear dentures.

"So that is why you two spoke with lisps!" Exclaimed Carlein.

But, we had parts of the Bible and we were all thrilled. After sitting down to read the pages out loud, they we talked about giving one page to the brothers next door. It only seemed fitting and so we decided to do just that for tomorrow's treat for the brothers. There had been a lot of excitement for this day and so after their meal and sleeping arrangements set up, we fell into a long, restful night's sleep.

Chapter Three

The men had been delighted to receive such a rich reward of a page from the Bible and they couldn't stop grinning and waving to the elderly sisters as they all went about their routine of, well, nothing.

It had been three weeks now since we had all been placed in this encampment and received the sections of the Bible. Those few words of encouragement had helped them all get through the days of no news from the outside world at all. None of us expected to be entertained but we had sort of thought something would happen, not this nothingness that was currently going on. Life was pretty boring. None of the guards, bringing their food, would even speak to them. They just brought the food, set it down and left. Then they would return an hour later for the empty trays. The medicine the different prisoners were taking had been confiscated by the military and yet each one of them had received their dosage with their morning meal each day. They would not starve to death nor would they die from lack of medicine so they were really perplexed about what *would* happen to them.

One day about a month after our incarceration, their meds came in small plastic disposable cups which the women decided to keep. We knew we were taking a chance keeping anything but when the next day came with no repercussions and our meds were in small sections of the tray again, we figured it was alright. So, the next time we were served a tomato and cucumber salad, we kept the seeds and planted them in the little cups just to give ourselves something to do. That is what we would do each day; tend to our little garden of eight plants. Four tomato and four cucumber plants. We had showed what we were doing to the brothers next door and they had done the same thing with their cups. It was just something to do to stop the monotony.

Then five weeks after our incarceration, one of the women woke up in tears. The group of women huddled about her and watched, unable to help as Frances wept bitterly into her skirt edging. She tried to speak to them but her tears were flowing uncontrollably and so Dolly sat down next to her to hug her. Katie sat on the other side of her as well. Finally, when Frances could stop the tears long enough, she began to explain that she knew her time had come and that her death was imminent. Shocked, all the women gathered around, dragging the lone cot over to sit upon.

"Frances, why are you saying this? What is happening that makes you feel you are dying?" asked Nathalie.

"Well, you know how right before you die, you become more active and more alert for a few days? Well, that is how I am feeling right now. My aches are gone and I feel better than I have in a long time. So, I know my time is near." she began to cry again.

"Wait a minute. Did you say you were feeling better now?"

asked Beverly.

"Yes." answered Frances and began to weep a little more again.

"Then I must be dying, also." replied Beverly. "I was wondering the same thing yesterday morning when I woke up without the usual aches and pains. I had so much energy that I walked around the compound three times. I figured I might as well enjoy my last few days or weeks or whatever. How about you girls?" She asked.

We women started thinking about the last few days and as our discussions within the group began to expand, our determination was that we were either all dying or something else was going on in which we had no control. Perhaps this was something we needed to ask the brothers about. So, we got another section of the envelope and wrote the query upon it asking if the brothers were experiencing the same thing as the sisters. Tying it within another mud packed ball, we tossed it up against the pole as before. Waiting anxiously for a reply while the men read our note, we clasped each others hands. We didn't have to wait too long as the brothers looked up after a small amount of time discussing things and nodded vigorously. Scribbling a reply back, the men tossed the mud pack back to the sisters side. I quickly grabbed the ball and cracked it open to read aloud to the other women, "it is time".

Gasping, the women looked up at the brothers and watched

the men nod solemnly. After those few moments of acknowledgment, things began to change for us all. We all started to pay closer attention to our own bodies to see the changes taking place gradually. Our strength was building up and we noticed our aches and pains were totally gone. We decided to experiment with one of us not taking our heart medicine once and when nothing happened, we then decided to just store the meds as they came in instead of taking them to see what would happen. Nothing was happening and yet we were beginning to feel better each day. After about a week of this, another strange thing began to happen.

One day, the soldiers forgot to bring breakfast to any of us. We all could hear activity in the distance but could not tell what was going on. Our lunch was delivered a little late but it was there and served by a soldier with a whopping black eye. The next day our dinner was not delivered and fighting was heard in the distance once more. The women and men gathered at the back fence to discuss what we should do and since there was so much noise coming from the soldiers, there was no fear we would be overheard. This was really the first time we were able to communicate so freely with each other, men and women.

"What do you brothers think is going on?" asked Dolly.

"We are not sure as yet but we believe that if you combine our improved health with their dissension, you have the makings of an approaching Armageddon. What do you think?" the tall, brother spoke.

"Oh, do you really believe it could be?" asked Katie.

"It is really the only thing that makes much sense to us."

Just then a young brother came running from their tent with a basket filled with grapes and bread. He was very excited about his treasure and his animated look of surprise sent chills up and down everyone's spine.

"Look what I found in our tent, my brothers." exclaimed the young brother.

"Where did this come from?" asked the tall brother.

"From inside the tent. I had to go put on my shirt so I could visit with the sisters and when I turned around to leave again, there was this basket sitting on the table. It wasn't there when I went in but it was when I turned around!" he exclaimed.

The tall brother turned to the sisters and said for them to check their tent as well. Linda rushed to their tent to return with a basket of grapes and bread also. She noticed something else in her basket and lifted the grapes. There was cheese nestled in there and she indicated the men should recheck theirs, also. Yes, there was cheese.

"Jehovah is providing for us. Yes, my sisters, the time is truly upon us, now. It is only a matter of time when it will be all over. By the way, my name is Jacob Frasier. This young man with the grapes is Henry Robbins." He finished the introductions of the rest of the brothers and the sisters introduced themselves as well. Grinning from ear to ear, we all sat down next to the fence and

48

shared our first meal together.

The next morning brought wonderful, miraculous changes to their camp. The seeds that we had planted had become fully mature plants that had worked their way into the soil and was producing tomatoes and cucumbers ripe for the picking. Our water supply, which was the large, dispensable, bottled kind the soldiers had placed in each tent, was full that morning despite the fact that no water replacement bottle had been delivered. A bowl of grapes and bread and cheese sat on the table as we rose for breakfast, causing smiles to come our faces. Our God, Jehovah was seeing to our needs. This assured us that the rest of the Witnesses, no matter where on the globe, were also being taken care of, as well.

We all met at the fence and the brothers offered up a prayer for our meal and to ask for Holy Spirit and the sanctification of Jehovah's name. It was heaven to hear, from the sister's standpoint as we truly missed hearing a prayer from a brother. Our hearts were so elated and our health was rapidly improving. It had now been eight weeks since we had been put in this camp and we were very happy to be where we were, both logistically and time-wise. We were enjoying our time away from the world and all its problems that we nearly forgot the world was still there. But the world reared its ugly head later that day after we had all eaten our lunches and were resting in the afternoon.

Several huge trucks entered the compound and soldiers jumped out of the back of each of the trucks. They lined up in front of the fence and one soldier stepped forward and commanded that the women come forth from their tent. We did so with much trepidation, slowly walking towards where the captain stood near the gate.

"We have been given orders to line you all up and shoot you. The extermination of you all is requested by the President himself. This goes for all of you people in every town, city and state. The purpose is to eliminate you all with speed. However, we here are not murderers. But we cannot allow you to remain alive. Our plan is to just leave. It would be more humane if we did shoot you but starving to death will at least allow you time to say your good-byes to each other. We are wiring the fence with electricity so you will not be able to leave. Our orders are to attend to the towns as chaos has arisen and we don't have time to coddle you with food and water. Here is a loaf of bread and a two liter bottle of water. Your last meal." He smirked a little and turned to leave. His troops proceeded to run wiring around the perimeter and after about an hour or so of attaching things here and there, they all climbed into the trucks and left. The women picked up the bread and water and proceeded to walk to the rear of the area behind their tent.

We marveled at the fact that the soldiers never even noticed the tomato or cucumber plants. They even brushed up against a vine that had grown out through the fence during the night and still they took no note. We women turned to where the brothers stood with the same look of perplexity we had. We were standing there staring at each other through the fence when the electric wire that had just been installed popped apart, ending their need to watch where they touched. With no connection to the source, there was no electricity running through the wire at all. The men and women just looked at each other and then began to grin. It was the knowledge that our lives were now under Jehovah's control that gave us the sense of true security and happiness. We all knew it was just a matter of time before the battle would be over. We felt the battle had begun and as the soldiers had stated; they had to fix the chaos.

The realization came that the war was in full force when explosions were heard in the distance and gunfire rang out and was returned. Screams were heard afar off but the battle did not come close to we in the compound. There was a loss of electricity. No more lights at night for us. The battle raged on for days and days. Inside the compound, life went on as usual. We got up to breakfast of grapes with cheese and bread and then tomato and cucumbers with bread and cheese for lunch and dinner. Our water source was never dry and we took to meeting at the fence each morning to start our day with a prayer and Bible reading. Even though we covered the two pages of scriptures over and over, it was wonderful to have even that much from Jehovah.

The group of prisoners never gave a thought to escaping at all. Inside the compound, we were safe. We were being taken care of by our God, Jehovah. He was providing our basic and elementary needs and He was improving our health on a daily basis. We could have been at one of the finer health spas for all we could tell. Our clothes never did wear out the whole time we were there. Even though one of the sisters had torn her skirt on a protruding nail in the tent house, the next day, it was repaired. Our shoes remained in good repair as well as our bedding. The rain barrels that were in each yard for bathing never ran out of water nor did it become stagnant. It reminded them of how God had taken care of the Israelites when they wandered in the wilderness for forty years without their clothes or shoes wearing out. All our needs were being met for the duration of the battle of Armageddon. We just had to wait it out.

Wait it out we did. After twelve weeks of incarceration, we awoke one morning to utter silence. Both groups of people in the compound came out at the same time to find the plants were gone. There, in their stead was a table with nine baskets of food in the women's compound and seven baskets in the men's compound. We looked at each other and then took our baskets around to the front of the tent area to where the gate was located. It stood wide open.! Our excitement was something that could nearly be felt as we all approached the gates. At first there was hesitation as it could have been some sort of trick. But when the eldest brother walked through their gate and nothing happened, we all filed out.

Both groups ran to each other and hugged each other. The

men and women had gotten to know each other really well during their time together, incarcerated. The women were elderly and had seemed to be like mothers to the younger men imprisoned. Our joy at being free at last took a back seat to the astonishment that came from seeing a wagon, with two horses pulling it, come around the bend where the soldiers had previously come from. No one was on the wagon, just the horses. It was an old fashioned buckboard straight from the old westerns the women used to watch on television. It headed straight for us and stopped just short of where we all stood.

"I take it this is our ride, wouldn't you say, sisters?" grinned Jacob.

"It looks good to me!" exclaimed Katie. We all agreed and the young brothers helped the older sisters climb up into the wagon where benches were set up. Their improved health made it so much easier to climb aboard. It was a large wagon and with two of the brothers sitting in front, that left room for the remaining fourteen people to sit in the back. The horses took off without assistance once they were all settled in and the brothers just let the horses have their lead. Apparently someone was leading us to where we needed to be.

Two more wagons full of people came around the bend as did the wagons for them and an assortment of women with children had climbed inside. They waved frantically at the other group and waves of joy were returned. Still, no one knew each other so some sort of organization had gone into the soldier's placement of them. The military didn't realize the bond that would have been between we strangers because of our faith was stronger, so their efforts to divide and conquer had failed.

Traveling out of the compound was so much more delightful and exciting then traveling in to it. We chattered away amongst ourselves until the wagon turned the last corner where a great deal of the battle had taken place. The sight was something horrendous to be seen, even though these people laying dead on the ground had declared themselves enemies of Jehovah. Yet, not one of the ones in the wagons could feel anything towards the ones laying there. It was just unpleasant. No tears were being shed. The horses kept moving. The ones inside the wagons decided, once they left some of the carnage behind, to eat some of their food.

It was very pleasant to ride along together and share a meal, prayed over by an older brother, Guy. He finished his prayer and began to check his basket for food. He pulled out a big chunk of wheat bread that had bits of cheese baked in it. There was some apples and figs along with some small carrots and celery for munching on. A jug of water had been found under the seat of the buckboard that had a ladle in it for drinking purposes and no one complained about drinking after anyone. It was such sweet water. We moseyed along like this for the better part of two hours, finishing our lunches and chatting away, speculating on this or that.

Wondering if the horses knew where they were going.

Our stomachs replete with good food, we could see we were approaching what used to be a large town. Nearly unrecognizable now with its destruction through looting and rampage, we did realize that it probably was what used to be known as Summerville.

What a difference Armageddon could make! What had seemed like a nice quiet country road was in fact Main Street. They were being delivered to the congregation of we sister's. The women looked at the men and asked them where they were from.

"Well, we are not a long way from home apparently. We live in West Ashley, but it is a different circuit from yours. I wonder if the horse plans to take us there once you sisters are dropped off?" asked Jacob.

"Yes, that will be interesting to know." stated Beverly. "I guess we will have to wait and see. Look there!"

There was the Kingdom Hall where many men and women were being gathered. Numerous modes of transportation included horse drawn carriages, bicycles, and many horses, saddled, were in the parking lot. The front doors were opened and candles were lit inside to provide light as there were no windows due to potential vandalism in the past. But that was over now and the horses drawing their wagon walked right up to the front door and stopped. Many people had been applauding as they had come forward so that sound increased as the elderly women were helped down out of the wagon by men who were standing there. As soon as the last sister was out, the horses started to move on again and so the brothers in the wagon shouted their farewells with hopes to see everyone again soon. Waves and blown kisses resounded in the air as the brothers wagon headed towards West Ashley.

The end."

Looking over to where Abigail had sat listening, Gail saw that she had slid down onto the rock below the stump and resting against the trunk, had fallen asleep. She smiled, picked up the child and took her inside to sleep in a more comfortable location.

Chapter Four

Josie's World

2016 A.D.

Josie, had left her faith for three years when reality struck her that she was not where she needed to be and she quickly made adjustments in her life to get reinstated. That was awhile back and she had been reinstated just nine short months when suddenly all things prophesied began to be fulfilled. She was nearly forty-five years of age and had three children; all a year apart, who were doing quite well in the Faith. They had their own families and she was about to become a grandmother for the first time. A grandmother at forty-five, unreal, she thought. Still, she was happy for her children and a bit sad that she had forsaken the truth for the amount of time she had. She was one of those women who think their sole purpose in life is to reproduce and raise their children till they are on their own and then they are of no further use. She supposed it was a kind of mental illness associated with an empty nest syndrome that allowed her to believe she was useless and to give up. The elders were so very kind and understanding when at last she came to them. They did all they could to allow her return to be swift and now her she was at the precipice of a whole new world and she was wondering if she had waited too late.

Many of the Witnesses were now in jail. The government had rendered all religions null and void so as to confiscate their funds and end religious wars. They had initially excluded the peaceful Witnesses from this course of action but towards the last few weeks, they started gathering the men together from this faith. With that action of suppressing them going before the Supreme Court as unconstitutional, the court had to side with the powerful government and moved it into the international arena of the United Nations to determine. At that point, it made it an international issue and thus all of Jehovah's Witnesses earth wide had to be disbanded. It had to be made to look correct. Now the country had a chance to regroup and grow back to being a world leader in economics. Or so they thought. This deed, of course, angered their God, Jehovah and it set in action, all the things that needed to take place for the battle of Armageddon.

Josie had watched all this unfold on International Television from a coffee shop in the small town in Florida, where she lived. Gasps were heard all around the room when the shocking news was announced. She looked up just in time to see a couple she recognized with their tiny, blonde haired daughter, Abigail rise from a booth and exit the shop. They were with her congregation and she knew she should be leaving as well. She slowly rose and looked around with feigned indifference. Then she left a large tip and smiled at her waitress so as to not draw attention to herself and waved bye to her. The waitress smiled back and waved good-bye back to her. Josie wasn't sure what was going down or what might be happening right now behind closed doors in politics but she knew it was time for all of them to gather together to find out what the next step would be. The brothers and sisters had all been told to meet at the homes of the book study groups should anything untoward happen and she turned her little Nissan down the lane to Brother Wesley's house.

A block before she got to it, she recognized a brother standing by the side of the road. He waved her down. He advised her to park right there and walk the rest of the way, as too many cars would draw attention to the home. Then he smiled and moved further along to stop the next car. Josie parked and walked the remaining block and walked quietly in the door without knocking. Any noise that would draw the attention of the neighbors was a no-no. Silence was heavy in the room, which already included about twelve people, including five children. The children were unusually quiet and seemed to understand the gravity of the situation. Several sisters stood and went to hug her and she felt their warmth and strength, which helped her tremendously. Two more sisters came in and then the brother who had acted as traffic guard stepped in the door to close it with a thud. He looked around the room and motioned for the rest of the brothers to come into another room with him. The remaining few of them looked around at each other and sighed heavily. What was happening, they wondered?

The land line telephone rang once and stopped. The group looked at each other pensively. Swallowing hard Josie decided to clear her throat. The small sound she made seemed to come out extraordinarily loud and everyone turned to her. She blushed and whispered she was sorry but all smiled and it seemed to help the rest of the group relax a little bit. There were four brothers in the other room, two of which were elders and two were ministerial servants. They were obviously on the telephone with others and the wait for them was becoming one of anxiety. Several children had to be hushed quickly and the two sisters who came in last, who were also fleshly sisters, held onto each others hands. Some noise from the other room heralded the brother's return and all looked anxiously at the door as it opened for the returning brothers.

"Well, my dear sisters, we have some instructions for us from the Faithful and Discreet Slave through our Circuit Overseer. Because we had advanced notice that this was shortly to take place, Brother Wesley has already been given supplies to cover our physical needs as well as our spiritual needs. Please drop your vehicle keys into the basket by the door so that we can take your cars and park them at the Mall. After all, the best place to hide a tree is in the forest, eh? You will not need your vehicles any more. Apparently there is a search about to take place for us thinking we will flee in our vehicles. I see you each brought your survival packs with you, so that in the event we have to split up later, you are prepared. That is good. I wanted to assure you all that your

60

families are all accounted for and safe. Brother Wesley has an interior room that is very large but with no windows where we will be gathered for a while. Apparently, they are not searching houses as yet. They are hoping to catch us out so as to arrest us on trumped up traffic charges. How long this will go on is anyone's guess. Please try to keep all noises at a bare minimum and whisper if you need to communicate with each other. I know it is going to be hard for the children but since none are under five years of age, we should be able to control the noise level somewhat. Now, here is the exciting news. This is it. The battle has now begun. Yes, my family, we are instructed to sit still and watch. It is unclear how long this will take and we have to be cautious but things have now progressed to beyond anything we have experienced to date. Any questions?"

"How are we to watch when there are no windows?" Brother Johnson asked.

"Oh, I'm sorry. I forgot to tell you about the television. It is just behind this screen." Carter rolled a screen away from the wall and a fifty-two inch television loomed in front of them all. He grabbed a remote and turned it on. Then he muted it, quickly.

"We can watch the news, both locally and internationally until the cable company shuts down. That will happen pretty soon since that will probably be one way in which Jehovah will confuse everyone and have them turn on each other, as prophesied." He explained. "Once it gets to that point, we will await more instructions if the telephone system is still available. If it isn't, I have been given instructions to play it by ear. Now, are we all settled?" he asked.

They all nodded their heads and turned their attention to the news on the television. The brothers had gone to deliver the vehicles to Mall and had returned safe. A great sense of calm seemed to permeate the room and even the children settled down to put a puzzle together. They knew that when something happened, they would be called back over. In the meantime, the news was boring to them. As one of the brothers surfed through some of the channels, he would pause if he saw the name "Jehovah's Witnesses" but more often than not, it just mentioned what they all already knew.

Josie sat in the corner, praying. She was very grateful she had made it to her group. The brothers and sisters were so wonderful to her and she had tried her best to be wonderful right back. She loved the entire congregation. Any doubts she had about whether she made it back in time fled when she was welcomed into this home on this day. This day of all days would be remembered in her mind for an eternity. She felt sure all others would agree. The day it all began. She briefly gave thought to her children, and then let it pass, as she knew they were fine. She would see them on the 'other side', she was sure.

They all settled down in the various chairs or sofas so they could relax as best they could. This was an intense time that had everyone holding his or her breath one minute and blowing it out the next when something exciting came on the television. They were all watching it when a news update came on over top the regular news. The sound was turned back on so all could hear it. Rioting had begun in all the larger cities throughout the world. Food was scarce and people were stampeding the grocery stores. Many injuries were reported along with several deaths. No one could explain the confusion, the reporter said, but he was going to be moving off the streets before he got hurt. Unfortunately, he was too late. A man came looming onto the television screen just then and slashed the reporter with a huge kitchen knife. The sisters in the room gasped and turned away from the screen. One of the brothers muted it again and turned to comfort his wife. All of them turned to each other with sad eyes and to comfort each other. What could one do, however? Plenty of warning had been given, just as in the days of Noah. No one would listen. Now it was too late.

Chapter Five

The hours turned to days as the television went dark and silent. The telephone service went dead just after the satellite service. The instructions given were to stay put if they were still safe and to not move at all. The food rations seemed to be holding up strong and water was plentiful. Once in a while one could hear someone outside yelling to someone else and then silence. The silence was eerie. They noticed there were no more airplanes flying above and they were near an airport. No automobiles were being heard anymore. The brothers decided, after a day of hearing nothing, to venture towards the front door with its glass panes. They advised the sisters to stay where they were and to not let anyone in unless they could verify it was the very ones leaving. They opened the door to the room and noticing the remainder of the house was empty of people, strode towards the front door. They started to go out the door but then one of them remembered the strict orders of the Faithful and Discreet Slave, which states that no one should separate themselves from the whole group until a sign was given.

They returned. It was important for all of them to move towards the outside together.

"Sisters, it is time for us all to go out the door." Said Brother Wesley. "Gather the children and let us see what has happened on the outside."

They all put on their survival backpacks just in case, and walked towards the door. It squeaked loudly against the silence that met them from the outside. The first thing that could be noticed was the smell. It smelled strongly of fresh blood. Everyone grabbed their face masks and put them on. Josie had never smelled anything like it in her entire life. She felt slightly nauseous. She knew for a certainty that nothing would ever be the same as it was before. Looking up and down the road, all she could see was bodies. Dead, bloody bodies of males, females and children. These people had killed each other right there in their neighborhood and they did not discriminate against women or children. Josie felt numb. She had to avert her eyes. Looking up towards the sky, she gasped. Everyone turned towards her at that point and all she could do was stare upwards. Everyone else finally turned to look at the sky. They all gasped.

What they all saw defied any logic to explain the phenomenon in the sky above. It glowed like the sun but it was many faceted like a diamond. It sparkled like a diamond, also. Every once in awhile, the face of a man would appear in one of the facets and then disappear, only to reappear on one of the other facets. It took up double the space of the sun, however, so therefore it nearly seemed to fill the sky. Its glow remained minimal so as not to compete with the actual sun, which was on its way towards a setting. The jewel began to emit a sound like a low hum. Then it played a musical note or two as on a piano. Suddenly a gentle voice could be heard starting in a whisper, progressively growing in volume until it was easily heard above all other noises. It kept repeating the same thing over and over. It said: "Please meet at the Kingdom Hall of your congregation". Then suddenly there was music. The Kingdom Melodies began to play. It was "Our Reason for Joy".

Josie and the others looked at each other and tried to focus on the task at hand. How to get to the Kingdom Hall. Obviously, they would not be able to drive there, as the roads were jammed with other vehicles and dead bodies. They were just going to have to walk.

"I think it is time, Brothers and Sisters, to get organized and prepare ourselves for the trek to the Hall. I know you are all feeling a little stunned at all that is taking place and the only thing I can think to do at this time is to offer a prayer of thanksgiving to our God, Jehovah. Let us then pray." Said Brother Wesley. They did.

By the time they reached within a mile of the Hall, they noticed other brothers and sisters straggling in from areas surrounding them. All were headed for the Kingdom Hall and so they all must have seen and heard what Josie had. Eyes, filled with relief and tears of joy, also glowed with spirit at discovering who was still alive and well. There was general chatter among everyone as more people joined the group, each with their own story of survival. One couple had gotten caught in the midst of the trouble when they just decided to stop and stand still, as advised. They said that they felt like a huge bubble had encompassed them and they had remained like that for three days without the need for food, water or rest. They were excited to share that experience. An entire family of six had somehow been transferred to the high branches of a huge oak tree where they spent their three days, without needing anything for survival. They had seen it all and were sharing their tale when they spotted the Kingdom Hall ahead.

There were three congregations that met at the one Hall. Josie and her children were part of one known as the East Congregation. Josie looked around hoping to see her children but they were not in sight as yet. She hoped they would get here soon as she was very anxious to hear their tale and share hers. It seemed that as many families there were, that was how many different accounts there were of their survival. Not one story was a duplicate situation. It was certainly going to make a good book for the new world, Josie thought. The one story that stood out in her mind that she had heard was the one with the seven year old girl who survived while the rest of her family did not. She was the study of one of the pioneers and had reached the point of dedication with a view to being baptized at the next assembly. She recalled how she had been playing dolls in the living room when her mother got angry and made her go to her own bedroom. Her mother had then locked the door, as she often did when upset at her, and walked away. The little girl started hearing many sounds like fighting but that was not unusual so she just went back to playing with her dolls. The next thing she knew was a brother opening her bedroom door and inviting her outside. It was three days later and she had been oblivious to time altogether. None of her family was anywhere to be seen and so she left with the brother to come to the Hall. She had been spared much of the trauma of Armageddon. What a wonderful God they all had, thought Josie.

"Can I have everyone's attention?" asked Brother Craig. All drew in closer to hear his comments.

"It seems that we are all here and accounted for with the exception of four or five so I will ask you all to move in to the Hall and find a seat. Some of you may choose to sit on the floor. As a matter of fact, why don't we allow the children this opportunity to sit on the floor up front and that will free up chairs for the adults. I know some of you are anxious and will want to stand. Feel free to do so. I cannot say as to whether we have any sort of conveniences like water or toilet usage so we are checking that out right now. I see most of you have survival packs with you so use them sparingly until we assess the situation. If everyone is ready, shall we go in and get started?"

The brothers and sisters starting filing into the Kingdom Hall and were guided where to sit by other brothers. Josie hung behind; as she hadn't seen her children arrive as yet. She was beginning to worry because no one had seen any of them and a slow dread began to fill her heart. As the seconds turned to minutes and the last of the group started to go into the Hall, Josie's heart began to weigh down, heavily. She turned to look down the road where she knew her children's homes were located and, seeing no one, turned back to go in to the Hall.

"Mom! Mom!" Josie heard. Turning swiftly towards the sound coming from the opposite direction she was looking, she saw her three children and their spouses hurrying towards her. They had their backpacks on and some were carrying small bundles in their arms. Then she noticed that her son-in-law was helping her oldest daughter along slowly. Oh no, Josie thought, she's hurt. How could that happen? She hurried towards her. A sudden cry drew her attention to the bundle in her daughter's arms and a quick glance spoke volumes. Seeing her daughter's glowing countenance and the proud papa's grin made Josie's mouth drop open in shock. Then she laughed and grabbed the mother and baby in her arms and hugged them till her daughter started to squirm.

"I went into labor a few hours ago, Mom. You wouldn't believe it! There we all were inside the house having lunch when the house seemed to seal itself. The walls became nearly invisible as we watched all the horror going on with Armageddon. It was the most amazing thing we ever experienced! I guess the excitement became too much for the baby and by the third day, he decided he wanted to come out and see what was going on. Mom,

69

I hardly felt a thing. I had this urge to go the bathroom and since we knew enough to have drawn water in the tub in case of an emergency, I instinctively climbed into it. It was so warm from the house's warmth that it was very comfortable and I felt safe. Josh followed me in to make sure I was all right and he helped me in the tub. Mom, it was the most amazing birth ever. Holy Spirit or angels must have guided Josh because he knew just what to do and before we knew it, our little boy was born. Mom, we are naming him Abel after the first man to have died as this is our first little man born on this side of Armageddon."

Josie nodded the whole way through the story as Josh interjected his portion here and there and her joy knew no bounds. Her family was safe and growing and a wonderful life was ahead of them. She wiped away more tears as a thought occurred to her. The children's father would be resurrected before much longer. Could life get any better than this? Josie didn't think so. But it would.

Chapter Six

The New World

2116 A.D.

a Patches was busy doing some sort of strange dance around the couple hoping to get in a few licks for her self.

"Nice work Patches! Whose side were you on, by the way? You are supposed to be pointing at Onyx, not me. Don't give me any excuses, either as I don't want to hear them."

"Still talking to your animals, Angie?" Said a voice from behind her.

"Oh, hello, Mom. Yeah, you know me. I have better conversations with my animal friends than some of my human friends. But, hey, if you tell anyone, I'll deny I said it." She laughed. She brushed the dust off the front of her shift and unbuttoned the flap that had converted her shift from a dress to pants and then back again when needed. She went to her mother, Ella and gave her a big hug.

"So, Mom, what's up? It must be important or you wouldn't have walked all this way. Is everything alright?" She asked.

"Everything is fine and I didn't walk. I rode. That is what I am doing here. I wanted to show you my new mode of transportation. Come back down to your house as I've the most exciting thing to show you."

"Well, lead on. Lets see what's up."

The two of them walked down the sloping path between saplings that created dappled shadows upon the pathway leading to Angie's home halfway to the bottom of the hill. She had created a winding pathway just for the shear joy of having diversity on her few acres. When she was given this land, her heart leaped with joy at the wonderful combination of both level and hilly aspects. She could let her imagination go wild with landscaping ideas and still have plenty of room for her animals she loved. One couldn't bind any animals in this new world in which they now lived but you could love them enough so that they stayed near. Angie had quite a few animals that loved her dearly and seldom left her side. Patches the tenth, was her pointer; Onyx was the panther, which couldn't get enough of the hunting games; Cloud, the beautiful snow white Arabian prancing around in her back meadow and Polymer, the blue and gold Macaw. Angie loved her inside joke of naming her bird Polymer because the silly thing loved crackers, hence the Polly part of her name but also loved swimming in the clear lake next to Angie's lot, hence the mermaid part of the name. So Polymer it was.

They rounded the corner of Angie's two-storied log home with its hollyhock borders to where her Mom had brought her new mode of transportation.

"You finished it!" Squealed Angie. "You finally figured

72

out a way to harness the ostrich?" They both quickly strode down to the barn about twenty yards from the house.

"Yes and believe you me when I tell you that it was nearly impossible. With Jehovah's help, though, I figured out a way to strap my sweet Petunia into a comfortable harness that could also support a larger, wicker buggy by going long instead of wide. She can't see its size and get panicky. The wicker makes it lightweight to pull. Angie, we can go so fast! Plus, I can carry more of my artwork to the festival now. I'm delighted and I just wanted to share it with you."

"This is really great, Mom. I'm so thrilled for you. I hope to see more of your work this year, then. I love the portrait you did of my animals and me. Hey, you have to figure out some way I can saddle Onyx so we can race."

"Hah! You can race me with Cloud. I don't think Onyx will ever stop trying to pounce on you long enough for you to get a saddle on him. Well, I have to go now. I have some artwork drying now and took this short break to show you Petunia's new outfit. I'm having a gathering next full moon, would you like to join us?" she asked.

"Sure, I'll be there. Want me to bring anything?"

"Naw, I've got it covered. Got some wonderful new recipes I want to try out before the big jubilee festival this fall. Hey, will you be seeing your Dad and Aunt Phyllis anytime before then? If you do, invite them over too."

73

"I see Daddy off and on when we happen to be at our borders at the same time so I will tell him. He will be excited to hear about your harness contraption. He's working on that sort of stuff all the time. His inventions are a big hit at the festivals. Expect him, ok? He and Aunt Phyllis are the best neighbors I could have."

"Will do, then. Okay, sweetie, give me a hug and I will let you get back to your animal hunt."

"Love you, Mom." Said Angie.

"Love you too." Angie's Mom climbed into the buggy with the highly plumbed ostrich and slapped the linen rope harness to request they move out. Their departure started slowly but then gained momentum until they were nearly flying across the meadow towards her mother's acreage closer to the ocean. Angie waited until they were just a dot on the horizon and then turned back to her house. It never ceased to amaze her how her mother could be twenty-four years older but look the same age as she. Living in the new world had brought her mother's youth back to her as well as Angie's. Angie had been forty-two when the great battle of Armageddon had started and she had just gotten baptized a few weeks prior. She was still eternally grateful her Mom had kept the kingdom hope in front of her. It was strange, though, how Angie's own daughter and son-in-law had taken to the truth before she did when she had been raised in the truth but left it in her teen years. Now, here they all were, enjoying the kingdom blessings and growing towards perfection.

Angie shook herself back to the present and began to walk slowly back to her house. She stopped about one hundred feet from her front door to look at the home she had helped build for herself once the clean up had been completed and the order was sent out that it time to start living life with gusto. She smiled. How she loved being in this new world with all its infinite possibilities. The battle was over nearly one hundred years now and she had learned so much. All the brothers who had been highly skilled professionals in the old system became instructors in the new world. Any technical college course you could think of was being taught at the learning center and these teachers were hands on. There would be a Jubilee Festival this year!

Walking over to the corner of her house, she ran her hand along the horizontal log that made up one of the beautiful beams of her log home she had actually taken part in building. She had helped strip the bark, had notched the ends and shellacked the finished interior. Recalling back to the day three elephants had been guided onto her property for the purpose of lifting the heavier logs, she threw her head back and laughed about the time the smaller elephant had wrapped his trunk around her waist to start to lift her. Angie wasn't having any of that as the elephant had already tried that on one of the brothers to accidentally drop him in a nearby mud puddle. Everyone laughed at that scene. What a fun day that had been all around. So many brothers and their wives

75

had taken part. Her Dad and her daughter Racheal had been there. Bobby, Racheal's husband had taken their three youngest children to his Mom's house for the day so that Racheal could take part for at least a small portion of the home build. Amelia, Racheal's eldest daughter and mother of her own five children had also helped. Stepping back away from her home, Angie looked up at the high center point of the chalet styled log home. She had carved her initials up there. This was her home and she was thrilled with all she had been given by Jehovah.

With Jehovah's help in the old system of things, Angie had grown accustomed to living alone with her dog. When the great battle took place, she and her dog survived. Of course, she was now living with the original Patches' offspring, Patches ten, so things had changed a little. But life in that old system had been a lot harder than she realized. At the time, it seemed fine. She had actually grown so used to chaos that it seemed to be the "norm" for her. She had moved in with her daughter for a while to help bridge the gap of moving away from an ex-boyfriend. It certainly had helped a great deal. Things started becoming a little bit better when her daughter had decided to investigate the Bible more thoroughly. Racheal had started exploring her spirituality by learning about Wicca. As time went on, however, she felt something was missing and there were too many questions left unanswered. Her grandmother had shown her some answers from her own Bible and that is when Racheal began to get excited by solving the mystery of it all. Playing her role as investigator, she delved deeply into the meanings of the prophesies of the Bible. Her boyfriend, Bobby was right by her side all the way. They actually had a lot of fun with it. It all started to make sense. Helping her mother escape from a doomed relationship was very satisfying to Racheal and jumping ahead of her mother's spiritual growth had a certain appeal. She hadn't realized how much her mother knew but had repressed. And she didn't realize how much her mother looked forward to a place she could call home. A place for her and her animals.

Angie loved her home and her animals. She had her daughter living just up the mountain from her and her mother was around the hill to her left. Her father, Maxwell, had been resurrected last year and owned a beautiful five acres further down the valley from her, which he shared with his sister, Phyllis. She loved being able to reacquaint herself with him. She looked much like him and when they walked through the lower valley village, people could tell they were related. She was only about two inches shorter than he and it gave her pause when she remembered she was only nine when he had died. She was sad for the lost years but oh so happy she now had an eternity to share with him. After all, he was a grandfather and great grandfather and great great...well, never mind, she thought, laughing to herself. It was all just too wonderful for words.

Just then, Onyx rounded the corner of the house with tail

switching back and forth. That meant he was ready for some exercise. Angie went into her house to change into her leather britches so that she could ride Cloud and give Onyx and Patches some running time. She loved this time of the day. It was just before the sun started to go down and the air seemed cooler and fresher. She went to her bedroom window, which was a one paned bay type window that overlooked the valley. It was such a long way down to the valley floor where many people brought their wares to exchange for whatever they needed. Still, you could see many homesteads that dotted the countryside in the valley and partway up the other mountain till the trees began hiding them. It reminded Angie of a postcard she had seen of Switzerland once. She noticed smoke coming from the chimney of her father's own log home and decided she would go visit him. Her animal entourage hadn't been to see him in several weeks so it was high time they visited him and his sister, Aunt Phyllis.

Angie came back out her house and saw Onyx and Patches laying peacefully on their sides in the shade of the porch. The porch was twelve feet wide that wrapped around the house. She levitated herself up the extra foot it would take to reach the ceiling fan to turn it on. She liked to have air stirring around her and the house was blocking the sweet breeze coming down the mountain. Coming back down she was suddenly alerted to some disturbance as Onyx and Patches both jumped to their feet with Patches' tail pointing straight back. Angie turned in the direction her dog pointed to see a tall man approaching in the distance. He was as tall as her brother, Maxwell, but his hair was very dark, nearly black. He was also a little more muscular, more like an athlete. His stride was long and he covered much ground as he walked purposefully towards her house. Angie became aware of how attractive he was as he came closer still. It was then she noticed the animal trotting alongside him. It was a magnificent spotted snow leopard. Angie was captivated, as was Onyx. As the man drew closer to her still, she speculated as to who he was and from whence he came. Only modesty kept her from saying something cheesy like "Where have you been all my life?". As he came up to her porch steps, he grinned from ear to ear and said "Where have you been all my life?"

Angie began to blush until she noticed that he was reaching down to speak to her panther. Oh, swell, she thought, losing out to a panther. But Onyx seemed to like the stranger and curled himself around his leg with his throat purring like a soft engine. The man reached down to scratch the panther behind the ears and then straightened upright, extending his hand out to introduce himself.

"Hello, sister. My name is Eric Landry. I live about three miles up the other side of the valley. I've heard from the brothers and sisters that you had one of the larger panthers hanging out with you and just wanted to see for myself. He is fabulous, isn't he?"

"Well, I sure do love him. He is so smart and such a lot of fun to be around. What about this snow leopard you have there?

Is it a he or she?" she asked, trying to keep him busy with conversation so he would stay a while.

"She. She traveled down from what used to be Canada when I was assigned to this area for clean up and we've been together ever since. I hope you don't mind me coming by without notice. We just started walking and our feet led us here. You have done some beautiful landscaping, by the way. It is very interesting. No wonder your panther likes it here. The boulders give him a high perch and the trails give him interests. Very nice. I must have you come help me figure out what to do with my lot. If that is OK with you?"

"Sure, no problem at all. I love figuring out what to do with something landscaping wise. What do you have now?" she asked.

"Not a lot is going on. I have a bit of a hill but nothing this grand. There are a lot more trees, however so I have some privacy. It is hard to explain. I hope you don't mind but I think I am going to swipe your idea of creating winding trails."

"No, swipe away. I think that is quite a compliment. We just love it here. We have no problem with privacy as no one has claimed the five acres just behind me yet. Perhaps I will plant some trees when that happens."

"Really? No one is back there yet? Hey, do you mind if I walk it? Would you care to show it to me?"

"Yeah, lets go look at it. Do you think you might be

interested? It would save me a lot of walking to your place to help you there." she grinned at him. He grinned back. She liked him a lot. He was so easy to talk with and had the most beautiful smile she'd ever seen.

They walked the area and spent a lot of time chatting and getting to know each other a little better. At one point they came upon a large boulder and he took her hand to help her up it. There was a connection there, Angie could feel it. He held her hand a little longer than necessary and she had no problem with that at all. Finally they finished their survey and Angie knew he would soon be her neighbor if he had anything to do with it. He told her he would get back to see her in a few days, if that was alright with her and she just nodded her head. He took her hand in farewell and bent to kiss it, following that with a grin and a wink. Angie felt her heart skip a beat but still managed to smile and say farewell without stumbling over words. Wow, she thought. What a sweetheart.

Her animals came back up to her side after Eric shooed them away from following him. She waved her thanks and then turned to get back to what she had planned on doing before this turn of events. She was definitely heading to her Dad's house now. She wanted to find out if he knew her visitor from any meetings.

Swinging her body up high with the help of the mane on her horse, Angie landed on Cloud's back with great, practiced ease. She whistled through her teeth for Patches, who came running at a gallop with Onyx loping alongside. Polymer took to flight from her perch and landed on Angie's shoulder. She wasn't going anywhere without them. The group wound their way down the valley through the tall pines that provided shade in this cooler time of the evening. As they slowly made their way around curve after curve, she glanced to her right as they went past her brother, Max Jr's home. She saw him in his garden with a snowy white cock-a-too resting on his shoulder and waved frantically to show him she loved him. He waved frantically back with a huge smile. Angie rode into her father's yard to dismount. A door to the house opened and Angie looked up.

"Daddy!"

Chapter Seven

Removing the tray of starter plants from the potting bench, Ella placed it on a five-tiered rack of plants positioned at a south facing window of her nursery. Ella loved growing things and since the new world was here at last, she took to experimenting with cross-pollination. She had accidentally managed to create a wonderful luminescence plant when she had fertilized some ferns with the remains of some glow-in-the-dark neon tetras caught in a tidal pool several months ago. She hadn't been able to duplicate the process but the plants themselves had kept true to that error and their seeds and cuttings grew into ferns that glowed in the dark. She used these ferns to border her pathways around her home and property. Most of the ferns grew to a height of four feet so it was quite a beautiful sight to see at night. She also suspected that the old phosphorus mines in the area might have helped create that bright greenish glow. Whatever the case, it was beautiful at night. Ella gave all the credit to Jehovah.

She stepped out of her plant nursery and gazed around. The giant, live oak tree she lived in had provided shade for her greenhouse while reflecting mirrors brought sunlight in from the yard. Grabbing a broom she had made from corn husks in the summer, Ella swept away some of the acorns that the squirrels hadn't stored away as yet. While she swept, she thought back to how she came to live in the oak tree.

Ella had been on the run from authorities that were gathering up the witnesses to put them in camps. A war had broken out in Asia and the US government decided to enlist anyone who could support the war. The campaign even included older people to help with cooking and cleaning so as to free up the youth. However, the witnesses were remaining neutral with the results that most were in camps under arrest with no trial date set.

Many witnesses were able to escape before being taken captive and the woods had become a hiding place for these with campers or tents. The need for water had prompted most to camp near the rivers. There were at least three inter-coastal rivers in the area that stretched for miles. This made it possible for many to remain hidden. Ella had a small camper in which she had stockpiled enough food to survive six months. The one thing no one counted on was the natural disasters that were part of the sign of the conclusion of the system. A hurricane had forced many away from the river and upon her return to the huge oak tree where she had previously stayed, she discovered a scene that could have come from the book *Swiss Family Robinson.*

The storm had torn up someone's privacy fence and tossed sections of it up into the tree creating the look of floors on two limbs. That was all the inspiration Ella needed to create her dream home in the new world. But the new world had been six months in to the future and rescue workers had meanwhile found her and several others. All were ushered into a fenced city of tents where they were kept until the great tribulation was finally over with the battle of Armageddon. It had not been as bad as she thought it would be. They were fed each day but only twice. There was a doctor on call for any health concerns so medicine was available. Since the only ones there were witnesses, it was comforting and up building in many ways.

Then came the day everyone had been waiting for. The start of the great battle. There had been a group of around seven angry men standing at the fence shouting obscenities to the brothers who stood as guards over the interior group. One man had picked up a broken bottle to hurl over the fence at them when a bolt of electricity shot out from a rolling ball of lightening and the man was incinerated on the spot. The rest of the men screamed and dispersed in all directions. The rolling, brilliant ball lightening split and followed each one. After that, screams of terror could be heard throughout the city. Meanwhile, the brothers quickly called for all to gather in the courtyard for a prayer. Everyone was frightened as nothing like this had ever happened and the group knew they were witnessing the start of Armageddon.

While an earthquake to top all previous earthquakes struck, the witnesses could only observe as they were locked in their tent city. The main city with its concrete high rises and office buildings began to sway back and forth like seaweed in a strong current. The sun was starting to go down and where there were usually lights beginning to flicker on, all there were was sparks flying and fire flare-ups from gas leaks. Buildings began to crumble and fall. Many people would be buried alive in that mess. The earthquake continued rumbling until it had destroyed every vestige of human construction. The silence thereafter seemed eerie and strange. The constant noise of traffic no longer penetrated the air. There was silence in the skies, which was unusual due to an airport located just outside the city.

The witnesses huddled in their courtyard numbered a little over two thousand. Over five hundred camping tents had been erected with four or five people or families sleeping in each tent. Now they stood in a large group staring out into the world gone mad, seemingly. As they stood there just looking, the huge, double gates snapped open, miraculously. No doubt angels were at work now. That meant it was time to leave.

Thousand upon thousands of slain bodies were all around with carrion birds already picking at the flesh. The odor was strong and putrid. Never before and never again would anyone witness a sight such as this. The brothers and sisters divided into groups consisting of their congregations and proceeded to go to their respective Kingdom Halls. It would have to go down in history as both the saddest and yet most gloriously victorious day as Jehovah's name was truly sanctified.

Ella's reflection came to a sudden halt when she heard someone call her name. Coming out from behind her greenhouse, she saw her friend wave to her. She waved back and watched as Gail, who had moved her from the Charleston area, made her way down the pathway of ferns. Many oaks created dappled light in the front of her house but she had cleared away a large area for a garden down by the river. She even had room for a tiny tea plantation. The river only ran past her tree house for about a mile before it opened out into the ocean, giving Ella beach access and dolphin playing fun.

"Hi, Gail! To what do I owe this pleasure?" Asked Ella.

"Well, Jim got called away to a new home construction and my services were not needed. My niece, Abigail just left to resume her duties as new world coach, so I came to see my best friend." Gail replied.

"Great! Can you stay the night, by any chance?" Ella asked.

"Sure can. I plan on it, even. You know me; I don't like traveling at night. Can I ask you why you have stairs when we can levitate up to the different rooms of your tree house?" Asked Gail.

"They aren't really steps. They are just different levels where I can perch to view my surroundings. Did that throw you for a loop when we discovered the same technique for walking on water also allowed us to levitate? Mind over matter and all that"

"It sure did. Faith is a much more powerful tool than I realized." Answered Gail.

"I can hardly wait for the sun to go down totally so you can see what I've done to the place." Remarked Ella.

"Wouldn't it help to have daylight to see?" Asked Gail.

"Wait and see and be amazed!" Grinned Ella.

As Ella and Gail swung on Ella's porch swing, sipping some tea from her tea plants, they watched the sun slowly creep down behind the horizon. Lightening bugs started sending out their tiny-lighted messages to mates. Ella's pathway took on a slightly greenish glow that intensified the darker it got. The leafy fronds swayed gracefully in the cool evening breeze, which created the oddest effect on the plants and pathways around the ferns. Gail's mouth opened wide with surprise and delight as the soft glowing plant life cast light all around the yard and tree house.

"Oh, Ella, how beautiful this is. How in the world did you get this to happen?" Gail wondered.

"Wish I knew. It was an accident in my grafting shed. I was propagating different plants including these ferns. I had some soil, which I got from the old phosphorus mine and was also using the neon tetras that washed up along the coast and got trapped in a pool and died. That was my fertilizer for the start of new plants and when they started growing, they started glowing. You should have seen my reaction when I came out to see the little shoots glowing in the dark one night. It is amazing! And I have some small starts for you to take home with you so don't worry." Ella explained.

"Wonderful! Jim will go nuts when he sees them. You

know, of course, that everyone will be wanting some of their own, right?"

"I've already thought of that and have a whole batch of pots waiting to be filled to dispense. Isn't Jehovah just the most wonderful God in the world?" Ella laughingly queried.

"I'd say." Replied Gail, laughing also. "And they grow so tall and strong. When he said he would make the soil yield its rich increase, he wasn't kidding around, was he?"

"No he wasn't. I plan to take a bunch to the festival when it comes time. I hope I can exchange some of these for some cooking pots. I also need a large container for making goat's milk soap. Clarabelle just had a kid and I will be taking the kid off her soon so as to get her milk. The fallen branches from this beautiful old oak tree will make lovely lye and I have saved assorted blossoms from my flowerbed for scenting oils. With the plants and the soap, I should be able to find someone with pots to trade, right?"

Gail grinned at her before nodding her head.

"So how are Max and Angie doing these days?" Gail asked her.

"They are doing real well. Angie has recently met someone very nice. Max, of course has yet to find someone but Angie's first husband helped her give me one granddaughter. I would love to see them both settled with mates and then I will have more subjects for my portraits." she grinned.

Ella was always in creative mode. From her garden to her animals to her artwork, Ella never came out of the creative mode. That must be why she seldom had time to explore the possibility of finding a mate for herself. Her life was so complete that a man would only compete and that was unacceptable to Ella. Gail shook her head and said a little prayer to Jehovah that she would always be happy.

Breakfast the next morning took place under the thatched canopy on the ground next to Ella's baking oven. Ella had placed a large round loaf of sweet bread on the table next to a ball of herbal butter and some soft cheeses. Next to that was a large bowl of assorted fruits and tomatoes. Ella knew Gail loved tomato and cheese sandwiches so this would be a treat for her. They sat there chatting away for a while and then cleared everything away. The leftover food was always left out for the animals that might pass by, as storage of food was not necessary due to its abundance. It never went to waste, as animals loved Ella's food as much as she did. Ella had a spring house over a spring that kept most things chilled before eating but it was wise to keep that storage at a minimum. It came in handy when Ella had a get together however.

She hugged Gail good-bye and they promised to let the other one know if they heard about any of their siblings or parents getting resurrected. The resurrection had started eighty years ago but their families had not been in the truth so they would be resurrected later. Ella's son, Brian, was due to be resurrected any time and she looked forward to that with much anticipation. She recalled the last few days of his life with a mixture of sadness and joy. He was such a funny little boy, only three and a half years old when he died, suddenly. They said it was probably pneumonia but when many children started dying from the same symptoms, it became its own disease of Reyes Syndrome. He became lethargic and threw up some white, milky substance, went into a coma and was dead within sixteen hours of the first sign of illness. Ella could only hold on to the resurrection hope as a means of saving her sanity, her loss was so supreme. Then her thoughts turned to a couple of nights before he got sick when she was trying to put him down for bedtime. He kept trying to delay her by making her tell him stories and then calling out goodnight over and over again. She had come back up the stairs to tuck him in one last time and he stuck his hand out and said, "Take my big ole hand". Ella laughed so hard because that was his favorite phrase at the time. Everything was "big ole". From the "big ole" truck to the "big ole" dog to the "big ole" shoe, it was all "big ole." Sighing now, she waved a final wave to Gail and went back up to make her bed.

Gail had slept in one of the three guest rooms she had built in the tree house. The tree had many branches in it that could support a twelve by twelve room if one added a few extra trusses here and there. Each room had a tiny, railed porch so as to make sure you didn't just walk out and drop. Within the rooms there was just a bed and a chest of drawers for overnight guests who may be

91

passing through. There was a pitcher and bowl for water and a few hooks on which to hang garments. It was just as nice as any bed and breakfast Ella had ever stayed in, she felt sure. She always had a floral arrangement ready in each room and soaps with towels were kept on the bed. Most guests carried something in exchange for the room and it always delighted Ella to see what they left as she knew it would be something she probably didn't have but could use. One couple had left two small wooden barrels that Ella used for making smaller quantities of wine. After putting in fresh towels and soap, Ella shut the door to the room and glided back down to her greenhouse.

Barely had a few days passed when word got out about Ella's ferns. After spending so much time exchanging many offerings for plants, Ella decided to just put the massive amounts of starter plants out at the end of the pathway and let any who wanted one, take it and leave their gift there. She had a lot of work to do and needed to get on with it.

"Excuse me, but could I have a word with you?" Said a deep, masculine voice.

Ella turned around to see a nice looking, tall man standing under her tree house holding an orchid. He looked so strange to her that she smiled a little at her thoughts. This was a very large man with large muscles and strong hands holding a very delicate, purple orchid that seemed to have a special aura around it. Curious, she stepped forward to give the usual greeting of a hug and then said "Sure thing. What can I do for you?"

"It seems you and I have been working on a similar project of botany. Your ferns glow in the dark. My orchids do also. So, I was wondering if you would mind sharing your story and a fern in exchange for an orchid?"

"Oh, your orchid glows in the dark? How wonderful! You have a deal. Won't you come in my greenhouse and see what I have done? This is so great to have someone to talk with who understands. Tell me, how did you get your orchid to glow?"

"No you don't! Your story first." He laughed. "I will tell you mine when you're finished." Ella liked his laugh. It was deep and genuine. She took a side ways look at him while he walked beside her to the greenhouse. She liked what she saw, too. He looked vaguely familiar to her for some reason. Looking down at his hand she noticed the absence of a wedding ring so he was either single or didn't like rings. What was she thinking? She wasn't looking, she reminded herself.

"Here we are. Feel free to take a look around and you can ask me anything you want. In the meantime I will tell you my story." She said and did. By the time she was finished telling him, she felt very comfortable in his presence. At her urging, he told her his story, which came close to matching her own. It was just a fluke accident. What made his so special, Ella felt, was that his was flowers with different colors that glowed. She was very excited to see it after dark. She looked longingly at the purple orchid he brought. He noticed her look and smiled, knowingly.

"That orchid is here for an exchange for your ferns, you know." He said. "By the way, allow me to introduce myself. My name is Clark. Clark Weller."

Ella gasped when she realized who he was. He had been a famous TV star on television. She used to love watching his Western on TV. She was thrilled to meet him but suddenly embarrassed. She could only stare at him, speechless. His slow grin told her she needed to shut her mouth and try to say something intelligent, which may have been asking too much. She dropped her gaze and began muttering about phosphorous and then got real busy brushing the dirt off her potting table. His hand reached out to take hers and he simply stated that he was glad he was alive and that his life had become the normal kind of life he had longed for in the past. She nodded and smiled.

They talked about their projects for what seemed like hours. Ella served him some of her homegrown tea and some cinnamon rolls she had made earlier that day. They chatted on like they had been friends for a long time. Ella figured it was because she could relax around him since she felt she knew him from his TV show and therefore lost some of her shyness. They really had a lot in common, she realized. He spoke seven languages while she only spoke three. They knew eventually there would be one common language but each language they had learned had its own beauty and nuances. Ella didn't realize how much time had gone by until her stomach growled it was hungry. They laughed and Clark took that as his clue that he needed to head towards his own home and dinner.

"Listen, Ella, I live about two miles further up the river, away from the beach. I, too have a tree house that I live in. I guess you usually travel to the festivals via the shoreline so you've never been up that way much. I'd like you to come see my work one day, if you would like. In the meantime, thank you for a lovely day and the ferns. I really appreciate it."

"You are quite welcome, Clark. It has been quite enjoyable, altogether. I'm so pleased you are working on orchids. I love flowers and had wondered if I would be able to do something with them but now I don't have to as you've already done it. Thank you so much. Perhaps we can do this again sometime." Said Ella.

"Yes, that would be great. I will see you soon then. Good-bye."

Ella watched him walk up her fern lined path to climb into a cart. She gasped when she saw that his cart was hitched to an ostrich. Why, she used an ostrich, too, with her cart. How amazing this was. To find someone who was so in tune with your self was truly phenomenal. She liked him so much. She hoped he liked her enough to return. She had found out that he was not attached to anyone and had been too busy with his gardening that he hadn't taken any time out to find someone. He said he figured it would just happen one day and as Ella thought back to the events of the day, she hoped he would return and allow it to "happen" with her. She smiled a smile that was filled with anticipation and excitement. He was so good-looking and smart and sweet. Well, most brothers in the new world were good looking and smart and sweet. She just shrugged and climbed into her bed after enjoying a light supper. The glow from the ferns created a type of night light so when it came time for her to levitate to her bedroom, she had no problems finding it in the dark. She had brought the orchid up to her bedroom and decided it had found its permanent home by her bed where she could look at it anytime she wanted.

Chapter Eight
Joe and Violet

Violet pulled into her garage without making a sound. She hopped off her Maglev vehicle and grabbed the two baskets she had bargained for when she went to the market center that morning. Violet had taken three of her paintings there in hopes that someone wanted a seascape or two so she could get the baskets. She needed the baskets to hold some of her harvest of grapes. She grinned as she recalled the response to one of her paintings of a bunch of grapes surrounded by some citrus fruit. A new and delicious drink had come upon the scene of late. It was made up of grapes and mangoes and something the developer wouldn't share with her but when he went nuts for her painting of grapes, mangoes and oranges, Violet thought she had an inkling of an idea. He happened to have some baskets she needed and she had her painting he loved. They bartered. That was the way it was done in this new world.

She looked back at her vehicle with some pride. She had wanted a Maglev vehicle ever since the local geniuses discovered a way to adapt the vehicle to the earth's magnetic field. Recalling her history lesson where the Germans had thought of the concept in 1937, got it patented but very little was done with it to the extent that it would become what it was now. She thought about how those developers would really be surprised at the adaptation of their design to just plain, old, ordinary dirt. Well, the iron ore in the plain, old, ordinary dirt. Using the magnetic fields and harnessing the power generated by it, an environmentally approved vehicle had been created. A vehicle made from old auto parts. No more walking everywhere. Although Violet loved riding her horse and giraffe, there were times when she needed to haul things to the market that would be too much of a burden for her animal friends. Plus her vehicle was clocked at thirty five miles per hour, which cut back on a lot of time. The cool thing was the safety issue. If you got too close to someone else, they created a field that forced the two away from each other. It took time to get used to but it was easy to control now. Plus keeping the speed limit to thirty five miles per hour helped to prevent accidents.

Looking around her kitchen, she found a spot below a cupboard where she could store the baskets when not in use. She was so looking forward to the harvest this year. The one hundredth anniversary of Armageddon, or Jubilee celebration with their first fruits was one of great joy and merriment. Although it was solemn at the beginning of the festivities due to thanking Jehovah for blessing the earth's production, it would work its way into a wonderful and happy festival. The Family, as they now called themselves, would gather in a big meadow and set up banquet tables for the great meal. She recalled last year's festival. It was most wonderful. Although Jehovah didn't require actual sacrifices anymore, they had wanted to show Him how well the paradise earth was producing. All right, it was an excuse to celebrate life and see old friends. Still, each brought something from their harvest to use as part of the meal for them all. Last year Violet had made saucer sized cinnamon buns that dripped with butter, honey and cinnamon. They no longer had to worry about weight gain so they reveled in the sweet decadence. She wasn't sure what to bring this year so she set about going through her cookbooks.

As the light began to fade on the pink and red swathed horizon, Violet decided it was about time to be getting ready for bed. Her usual ritual included shutting her windows and doors. She had learned her lesson the hard way right after Armageddon when she excitedly left her doors and windows open of the remaining homes that they used temporarily. The next morning when she had awakened, every furry creature you could name surrounded her. They wanted her warmth and comfort, she supposed. Anyway, she took to shutting her doors and windows just for the sake of a good night's sleep. Settling down, Violet tried to concentrate on what she would bring to the jubilee festival. It was only a month away and if she was going to do something fantastic to show her friends how much she loved them, she had better come up with something soon. And of course that was her last thought before sleep overtook her busy mind and shut her plans down for another day's scrutiny. The last thing she heard was the busy sound of crickets rubbing their legs together as lightning bugs darted about the yard adding a warm glow that nearly rivaled the moon's.

***

It had been one hundred years since that great battle of Armageddon. It had only taken twenty years of work for the survivors to bring the earth back to its original splendor. Nature had helped a great deal, of course. It amazed everyone that if you left something alone and did not do maintenance on it, it would pretty much dissolve by itself. All the wooden houses slowly crumbled into fine garden soil with the aid of maggots and other insects useful for the task. Plant life did what it did best and multiplied to adorn the earth with its beauty and grace. The earth yielded the best and the best only. Huge flower blossoms adorned most of the bushes and trees that grew in the park the earth had become.

The people now, that was a different story. They figured God was going to just plop a garden in their midst but that wasn't what he promised. They were the caretakers of the earth and had a big mess to clean up before it would grow back to the garden like state of Adam and Eve's time. They thought they would wake up one morning and the paradise would be there. It didn't take long for all to realize that if Jehovah did it, they wouldn't appreciate their work as much and in doing it themselves, they could decide what went where. They had been assigned their own lots to clean and plant and then been given common areas to attend to for those resurrected. The resurrection began about eighty years ago. Violet had lost a set of twin girls during her delivery and had looked forward to their return. She hadn't been able to conceive again in the old world but she and her husband planned for many in the new world, perhaps. When her daughters were brought to her swaddled in fine soft linen, she burst into tears. Her husband, Joe, currently away on a quick build home, hugged them all and cried without let up for so long. Of course the twins were close to fifty years old now. They both had concentrated on becoming teachers of other resurrected ones. There was a great need for that and they both put off settling down in marriage until they had put in some time helping.

Noah, Moses, Abraham and many others had recently returned. They had so much to share with all. They would travel the earth to share their stories first and later would set up their own household when they were finished that. Solomon's wisdom had not diminished one bit at his death. He was still the wisest man on earth. Violet had tried to pry some of his wisdom towards her but he just laughed and told her that he shared his brain with no one.

All in all, everything was falling into place naturally. Even people who had committed crimes would be resurrected soon. Most criminals or bad people were a result of the old system with little chance at a normal life. Now, they could reform. This would be a challenge, it was agreed. So many different religions and so many ideas of where you go when you die flourished among the

101

currently dead. But it would be exciting work and just seeing the amazement in their eyes at the new world was a site to be treasured. Violet and Joe had built their home with the idea that they should be able to house a few guests from the resurrected before their education was to start. Then they would go to school, of course. Once that task was finished in a few hundred years, Joe and Violet would think about having their own children once again. They knew that it would only take so many to fill the earth so they had prayed to Jehovah to allow them to have at least six children to contribute. They would have to wait and see if God's plans may have been adjusted where this would be allowed.

The house they had built rested on the five acres they were allotted. With communal gardens set aside in each area for raising crops like wheat and corn that required a larger growing area, the five acres would suffice for their individual needs. If you were single, you got three acres. Married, you got five. It was that way to make sure there was enough land to go around and two can live as easily on five as six. Joe and Violet's land was situated with part of it going up a gentle slope on the side of a hill five miles from the ocean. That is where they had planted their vineyard. The house stood at the front of the property and it was a grand Victorian style log home. This was a popular plan that many people had built when it was their turn to have a house built. It had a root cellar and an attic. There were six bedrooms on the second floor; each with their own bath. The master suite was on the main floor along with the kitchen, dining, living room and art studio. Violet and Joe were both artists and worked well together.

Violet had used the warm attic as a place to dry her herbs for cooking and soap making. It always smelled wonderful and lent its odor to the rest of the house. The basement or root cellar housed all the root vegetables grown during the year. They kept potatoes, carrots, rutabagas and sweet potatoes there. It also housed all the jars upon jars of canned veggies and fruit they needed when the growing season was finished and the ground rested till spring. These jars had survived the battle like any spoils of war.

Violet didn't know if she would ever get used to being awakened by the sunrise with its brilliant sphere aglow with purple and orange streaks of light. It never ceased to amaze her that she was here, really here. Jehovah's undeserved kindness was working overtime, she thought as she swung her feet down to rest them on the highly polished wood floors that morning. She had a wonderful plan of blueberry tarts and decided that would be her gift of food this year for the harvest celebration. She had canned thirty quarts of blueberries that summer and knew she had enough for all the tarts she needed to make. She would start on the shells today so that she would be finished before Joe returned in a few days. That would give her something to do. Her mind raced forward to the part in her recipe where she would be able to add her special touch of sweetened cream cheese at the bottom of each tart shell as a surprise. Mmm there was nothing better than cream cheese with blueberry pie. Her mouth watered as she thought about it.

Chapter Nine

Joe put down his hammer for a few minutes to pick up a cool drink his niece, Abigail had supplied. As he drank his lemonade, he did a quick inspection of the work the brothers had accomplished on this housing project. One of the sisters who decided she would prefer to remain single had become the main focus of the build this month. Although they worked quickly, it would take at least a month to build each house with the logs they used in this area. Pine trees grew quickly and were in plenty as sections had been cut to allow new growth. Other parts of the world used what was indigenous to their area for housing. Joe thought back to last year when he traveled north a few weeks to help build a home there. They had used stone in that area, due to its abundance. Now that was a house that would stand for a long time.

Looking back at the home he was currently working on, he decided it was nice but not as nice as his. Perhaps it had more to do with Violet living there with him. He smiled when he thought of her. She was always so excited about life and charged ahead with full gusto. Her mind was constantly running ahead to her next project. He was sort of like that himself. He had been working on a chest of drawers for Violet in his workshop above the barn. He kept it locked so she wouldn't snoop. She never mentioned it being locked at all so perhaps she hadn't noticed. Well, he was making a chest of drawers that would be embellished with hand carvings he had learned to do when working with a brother two projects ago. His excitement was due to the fact that he only had some tiny touch-ups to do and then he would be able to present it to her. He knew she would love it. This house he was working on now only had three bedrooms of which two were for guests. The sister living here spent most of her time with the animals. She loved them very much and worked with them daily to teach them tricks or working skills where they could be useful. She was the one who had trained Violet's giraffe to accept a girth for riding. A girth or belt and a halter were all that was needed to ride any of the animals.

The animals were trained to go right or left with knee pressure and when you said "whoa", they would stop. Sometimes it would be so funny to watch this sister train animals. There was a certain bear for riding. She called him "Gus". He would be anxious to please and would try to anticipate her next command. He was wrong many times and this sister would often find herself tossed forward into his fur when he thought she wanted him to stop and she had wanted to go right. His sudden stop would have her grabbing the girth quickly as she felt herself propelled forward. She would laugh and hug him for his desire to be of service but she had to correct his training session, nonetheless. She was not alone in this, as many other animal trainers, both male and female, had to

106

go through the same thing with their animals.

Joe thought back to all the housing projects he had worked on since Armageddon. There were hundreds. The projects became fewer as more and more were resurrected and were able to assist then, also. It had been great fun working with all the wonderful brothers. They were eager to assist and train all who had no previous construction skills. He had been one who had skills to teach with his woodworking hobby he had had in the old world. Of course, now there were only hand tools for building. Joe didn't really miss electricity as much as he thought he would. In view of the fact that he had eternity before him, he could slow down and do it right. No one was in a rush. There was always temporary housing for those whose house was being built so they didn't apply pressure. The temporary housing came with the camping concept of the old world. The many campers left over from the old world might look funny hitched to a horse but at least it worked.

Applause resounded as a brother drove home the last peg that showed the hanging plaque with the sister's name on it above the door. Finished at last. Joe stretched his muscles and back as he put his tools in the cart of his Maglev vehicle. All the brothers had given each other hugs knowing that would be seeing each other again in six months or so. That was the average time between builds considering that so many brothers had been added into the equation. Putting in the last of his tools, Joe turned on his magnetic auto and set his mind on home. He hoped Violet had gotten the message that he would be returning earlier than planned and would have something wonderful simmering on the stove for his dinner. Violet was a creative chef that was for sure.

As Joe moved silently through the forest where the trees had been harvested for this project, he saw that the gardening family members had already replaced the trees with either more trees or fruit orchards. Since the work was being orchestrated by Jesus, it was an assured thing that whatever was being planted was through the governing body and inspired. It was also an assured thing that it would grow at great speed and lushness.

The planting side of creating the new world had proved fascinating to Joe. Once the ground had received blessings from Jehovah, it took on a life of its own. No longer part of the environment, weeds were now a thing of the past. Brambles no longer ripped at your pants legs. Roses had no thorns as did not berry bushes. Incubation time for seeds was all about the same amount of time that green beans had taken in the old world. A day or two and that was it. When starting plants indoor, it never ceased to amaze him how quickly the plants began their lives. A day or two and you had a new plant starting to take root in the very fertile soil. Trees grew at a more rapid rate than ever and that made it great for harvesting the fruit from those trees. The mighty oak tree grew at a slower rate and it was used for furniture, shade and their nuts for the squirrels. The flowering bushes retained their blossoms for a lot longer and only needed a six-week resting

108

period between blooming times.

Joe's arrival time was only an hour away and the excitement of seeing Violet again lent speed to his arrival time. He was about to pass the Meadow of Purples when he recalled why it was called that. He maneuvered his vehicle over to where he saw a particularly abundant growth of violets. They were thick with multicolored blooms but he wanted only the purple ones. He reached into his side pocket of his cargo pants and pulled out a packet of seeds. Oh good he sighed, he still had them. In his hand were tiny seeds he knew to be lavender as the sisters where he had just left sent them as a gift to Violet. They would grow purple flowers which would go with Violet's purple themed garden. But so would violets, Joe thought. Going over to a tree he pulled some lush green moss from around the rock by the tree. Moss would grow back quickly.

He pulled his camp shovel from his gear and dug up a section of violets placing them within the folds of the damp green moss. He put all that into his camping dinner plate and then tossed into the ground some of the lavender seeds. The rule was this: you take from the ground; you give back to the ground. He was happy with his haul and so would be Violet.

Violet heard the back door slam shut just moments before a huge bunch of violets were pushed under her nose. She exclaimed with joy and hugged Joe with all her heart. She loved purple flowers.

"You are home a day early!" she exclaimed

"Is that all I get? You're early? Is that all you have to say?" he stood with his hands on his hips and his feet spread apart like some tyrant.

"It is the best I can do for now because I must give my husband a proper greeting when he gets here." She claimed as she moved into his waiting arms. They laughed at her little joke. Their embrace and kiss was what poets write about. Their love had stood the test of time in the old world and now far into the new one.

***

Later on Violet began to take the blueberry tart shells from the oven to cool with the others she had taken out earlier. This was her last batch. She had made extra for them to have after dinner and she wanted his opinion of the tarts. He had exclaimed over them with gusto so she figured it was worth the hours she had put in to baking the shells. She would add the cream cheese and blueberries just before they left in the morning. It was an exciting time for them both.

Joe was anxious for Violet to see the chest of drawers he had made her and was finishing it when he heard her call to him. Grabbing the dust cover and slinging it over the chest, he answered her back and told her to come up stairs to see something.

When she arrived at the top of the stairs, she saw a large three foot by five foot box covered with a dust cloth. She walked up to it as Joe stood beside it with his hand stretched over it.

"And what is this might I ask?" Violet queried.

"My gift to you for putting up with me all year" said Joe.

"Well that was a task and a half, I must say." She joked with him because she was slightly nervous. She had never been good at receiving gifts but Joe was working very hard to break her of that habit.

"I know! That is why I made this for you to make up for all the trouble I've caused you."

"Joe, I was kidding!" she exclaimed

"I know, honey. Are you going to remove the cover? Tell me what you think."

Violet removed the dust cover and immediately squealed with delight at the sight of the gift. One reason was because she was even getting a gift and the other reason was because it was the most beautiful chest of drawers she had ever seen. The carving was intricate and detailed a great deal. Tiny scrolls of wood wove its way in and out of the design that quite obviously was violets. She cried into his shirt and hugged him with all her might. She then kissed him all over his face and finally his lips.

"Yes you are kissing me now but will you later?"

"What do you mean?" she asked.

"Well, you have to help me carry it downstairs." He grinned. She simply smacked him on the arm and then took his arm as he escorted her back down the stairs to her tarts cooling on the racks in her kitchen. She had never felt such love in her whole life except when she first began to understand Jehovah's love for her. Many of the survivors hadn't felt they should have survived but apparently Jehovah had their hearts pegged as worthy.

The next morning found Joe and Violet loading up the tarts to head for the jubilee festival. The smell of them would knock your socks off. She had worked hard making the cream cheese three days ago and having that cool spring so near had proved an excellent way in which to keep the cheese hard enough. Chips of ice had drifted down from some unknown source at the top of the mountain and its renewing flow had helped keep things cool in the spring.

This time they traveled in style. They had an old fashioned surrey and two horses pulled it along. The top cover kept the sun from their heads and kept the tarts cool. They both sat down and Joe turned to Violet as he gathered the reins.

"Oh, I meant to tell you that I saw our niece, Abigail at the build. She said she has been given an assignment as Life Coach in our area now and is thrilled to pieces." said Joe.

"Oh, I'm so happy for her, Joe. That is just perfect for her and us."

"So, are you ready for this?" he asked

"I'm ready for anything." She answered.

Chapter Ten

It was a Jubilee year. One hundred years since Armageddon. A bountiful, creative celebration gives everyone the opportunity to market, display or show off his or her talents to all in attendance. Maglevs are left at home and arrival into the valley had to be via animal or on foot. There, booths were set up for anyone interested in bartering something they had for something someone else brought. Many people enjoyed sharing special recipe dishes they had prepared for this occasion. It would be great fun, at the end of the day, to check to see what someone dropped into the swap bin for a pie, bartered. In other words, one offering a piece of pie might find a carved wooden animal or a crocheted doily in the swap bin in exchange. Value was placed on friendship, not on a monetary system filled with the pitfalls of greed like they had in the old system of things prior to Armageddon. Those days were long gone.

Max enjoyed this new world where Jesus reigned as King and he planned to enjoy the festival to the full this day. His favorite part was the group of musicians of whom he was a part, playing the guitar. He had the great joy of playing with a group who were primarily stringed instrumentalists. The group was lead by David of old. He used to be a king in his lifetime prior to the war but enjoyed the time now as a prime overseer and lute player.

Jonathan, King Saul's son, also played with the group, finding his skill on the harp most enjoyable. Three other brothers comprised the remainder of the group. They practiced once a week at week's end and their skill of composing and writing songs created an extensive repertoire.

As was usual for Max, his work on his land came first and foremost in his life. Music was secondary only to his home and his worship. Waking up that morning of the festival, Max felt an overwhelming sense of satisfaction in all that he had accomplished in his life so far. He had everything he could possibly want in his life. He loved how he had discovered a way in which to grow plants on a vertical landscaped design that afforded him much more growing space. He actually overproduced for being the only person in his household but he was then able to share his excess with those at the festival, which was enjoyable and satisfying. It was worth the extra effort to grow unusual vegetables to this area and watch the early arrivals rush to his booth to see what he brought this time around. Since it was the fall festival of the Jubilee year, he had cross pollinated some gourds and shaped them to grow in boxes so that they would become the shape of the box. A few weeks drying time and the seeds would become loose and create a rattling sound, when shaken. Thus, he made a new instrument for him to shake with the group. Smaller gourds were painted with different shades of blue and pink to be transformed into baby rattles. Presenting a rattle to a new mother gave his heart great joy. His booth was often divided between his veggies, toys and musical instruments he made.

He dressed rapidly and grabbed a biscuit his mother, Ella had made, from his pie safe; he hurried out his front door to prepare his trip to the festival. He had packed most everything in his buggy the day before. His wood shop produced some of the sweetest sounding children's pipes and stringed instruments in the area. The small guitars and lutes he made were perfect for the young starting players. All he had to do now was hitch the donkey to the front and climb aboard. This he did with excitement and a sense of anticipation. What joy would happen today, he thought? Grinning, he began his five mile journey into the city, which was previously in the area of Jacksonville in the old world.

Abigail tossed her long, blonde hair over her right shoulder as she climbed up onto the seat of her tiny goat cart. She was a delicate looking woman of only one hundred and three years of age and quite beautiful with her natural, long blonde curls and bright blue eyes that often hid behind the long black lashes surrounding them. Flowers abounded in her cart and baskets held multiple bouquets of autumn blooms of lilacs, peonies and roses. She had managed to work with her spring blooming plants long enough so that they would find a way to become year round blossoms for her to take to the festival and please everyone. The paradisaical conditions certainly helped on that score. They were her favorite flowers and their aroma was nearly overwhelming in her wicker

115

cart where she perched as she clicked for the two goats that were pulling her cart to get a move on. She didn't want to be late.

Max came up the well-worn path from around the bend to join another path coming from a perpendicular direction to discover one of the most beautiful women he'd ever seen, turning onto the path that he planned to take. She had just missed seeing him but not he, her. His breath caught at the sight of her and he pulled back on his reins in order to slow down his speedier donkey. He wanted to follow her so that he could get a longer and better look at this lovely lady. His heart started to race as he watched her from a slight distance, clicking at her goats. What a lovely sight he beheld. The sun was just coming up over the horizon and had caught the meadow in pools of golden sunlight and reflective glistening dewdrops. Her hair was a massive mound of pale blonde, nearly white, curls that cascaded down past her waist. Max's donkey was becoming restless at the slower pace and began to toss his head in frustration. Max knew he would have to come up with a solution to this situation and so he pulled his donkey over and set down the disk anchor so that his donkey could graze but not stray. He then took off at a slight jogging pace to catch up with the slower walking team of goats that were carrying away the woman he hoped to meet just now.

He had to break into a slight run in order to catch up with her and he called out when close enough so that she would stop. Abigail heard a man calling out to her and stopped her goat cart to

116

turn and see a most especially handsome man jogging towards her. His pale blonde hair rivaled her own and his blue eyes seemed to match hers in merriment as both seemed to find joy in meeting. He was quite tall and well shaped with a pale blue shirt that drew out the color of his eyes and nearly matched the sky behind him as she looked up into his eyes.

"Good morning, my brother. I wish I could give you a lift but as you see, I merely have a goat cart and they could not haul our weight." She smiled.

Max grinned, his dimples melting her heart. "No, I see not. That is fine as, you see, I have my own cart back there and a donkey pulls it. I just wanted to catch up with you so that I could arrange a passing of your cart without scaring your goats and avoid dumping your cart hopefully."

"Oh, well, that is really thoughtful of you. My name is Abigail and I am on my way to the festival this morning. And you are?"

"Hi, my name is Max. Pleased to meet you. You have some beautiful flowers to take and unusual for this time of the year."

"Thank you. Yes, I really had to train and adjust them over the past twenty-five years or so and this year they are at their best with both appearance and scent. Do you like flowers?" She asked.

"Oh, who doesn't? But these are so fragrant and beautiful. So, how do you want to work this? Can you pull up and over at the rest area just ahead? There is a picnic area and plenty of room for your cart. My donkey is restless to move on and even though I would love to stay and visit with you, I am sure we both have things to accomplish this morning."

"But of course I will. It was very nice meeting you and I appreciate your kindness with this matter. A couple of younger men went racing past me earlier stirring up dust which settled all over my flowers and me and I fear I must look a sight."

"A more lovely sight I have yet to see, I assure you."

"Well, thank you so much, Max. A more gallant brother I have yet to meet." She smiled and his heart stopped racing in order to do a back flip. He just had to find out more about her. The festival became a distant memory as his gaze at her became more intense and interested. She suddenly became aware of his attention and modesty made her look down into her lap. He saw this and cleared his throat.

"Perhaps we could set up next to each other at the festival and get to know each other better?" Max asked hopefully. Abigail quickly looked up and smiled.

"That would be lovely. Save me a spot next to you and I will be along shortly. In the meantime, let me move over at the rest area. It was nice to meet you." She said as he turned to jog back to his own cart.

Max climbed onto his own cart after setting the anchor back into it and slapped the reins to move his donkey back onto the dirt pathway. She must live close by in order to be using the same pathway as he, he thought. Most roads were wider due to frequent use but her being on the dirt pathway the same as he made him think she was a neighbor he missed meeting somehow. He hoped she was, that was for sure. He had put his woven straw cap back on when he got to the cart and this he tipped it at her as he went past. She smiled her radiant smile and thought once again what a thoughtful man he was. Her heart was doing a flutter dance that caused her stomach muscles to do a twitch or two of their own and she had to calm her nerves before starting her little goats back down the path. She had never experienced this before and she mused as to whether he felt anything for her like she did for him. He must do, she thought, as he invited her to set up next to him. She never thought she would meet someone and be so instantly attracted. She hoped he felt the same and the anticipation of their time spent together at the festival spread a warm glow throughout her heart.

Abigail came around the last bend in the pathway to see brightly colored banners flying all around the meadow where this festival was being held this season, not too far from the beach. It almost reminded her of the renaissance fairs she had read about in the history books at the Grand Hall Library. This festival was a lot cleaner and much more peaceful, she felt sure. She glanced around to see if she could find Max. She had noticed his donkey cart was a highly polished wood with dark blue trim and she hoped no one else had one like it, as she didn't want to spend a lot of time looking. Her flowers would soon start to droop if she didn't get them under her a canopy soon. She would ideally liked to have found a spot under a shade tree but she failed to mention that to Max and now she would have to set up her canopy. She was looking into the sunny areas of the festival when she heard her name called. Turning, she saw Max coming towards her with his long stride. He was taller than she by a foot and she had to lean way back to look up at him.

"Hey there! I hope you don't mind but I have to set up in the shade so that my instruments do not receive heat damage. Will that affect your flowers blooms?" He asked.

"No! This is perfect. I had wanted the shade myself. The blooms tend to wilt quicker in the heat of the sun. But, you know, today doesn't seem to be too bad, weather-wise, does it?"

"No, summer is over, I believe. Come with me." He led her through the sunlit part of the meadow and over to where a grove of trees extended out from the forest. There were quite a few booths set up already by some who came early enough to get the shady areas and Abigail hoped to get set up quickly. As if reading her thoughts, Max said he would help her set up as he had already set up his booth upon his arrival.

Chapter Eleven

2116

The Jubilee Celebration

There were at least three thousand people in the valley that day. The people who attended were mingling around the booths that stretched out over the bottom of the valley while their animals used for transport grazed on the slopes of the valley. Most were wearing the costume of the area where they had lived and the time frame in which they lived. So it wouldn't be unusual to see Roman togas among Edwardian apparel at all.

The day went by much too fast for Max and Abigail. They blended their lunches together and shared their backgrounds with each other. It was like they were on a pathway to togetherness and both knew it. As the afternoon wore on, their shared laughter and wit drew them closer. They seemed a natural fit.

"Abigail, I have really enjoyed getting to know you. I can't believe you live so close yet we've never met. I guess we both have been real busy. Would you think it presumptuous of me to ask if you would accompany me to the evening banquet and following dance?" Max asked.

"I would love to go, although I must confess that I have not danced in many years."

"Oh, I'm sorry. I forgot to tell you that I am playing in the band so would not be able to dance. What a shame. This is the first time that aspect of my playing has ever brought me any type of regret. That is interesting."

"You play with David and Jonathan?" Abigail asked.

"Why yes, why do you ask?"

"You are that Max?"

"Yes. Again, I say to you, why you ask?"

"Oh this is delicious! David is an ancestor of mine and he has been trying ever so hard to get me to agree to meet with you as he thinks we would really like each other." She said matter-of-factually.

"You are the distant niece he has been going on and on about?" Suddenly the coincidence of the situation got to them and they both began to laugh with delight.

"Now I know why my great uncle sent me down that barely used pathway. I usually come into the city's valley via the main thoroughfare but he talked me into taking the lesser used pathway under the guise of it being shorter and less traveled. He said my goat cart blocks traffic. I told him that I would try it once but that if I didn't get here in time that he would have to buy all my flowers. He agreed with a laugh and now I understand why he sent me that way. Max, I can only apologize profusely for my uncle's schemes."

"No need at all. I think it was brilliant and it worked. Well, I hope it worked. So, will you accompany me to the banquet then?" He asked once again.

"But, Max, if anyone sees us, they will put two and two together and presume we are a couple. I don't think you want the conversation at the meal to turn in that direction, do you?"

"It is too soon for you to know if you have feelings for me?" He asked her gently.

"Well, I...I...of course I have some feelings for you already. Don't you think it is too soon to know whether they are strong enough to face the crowd, however?" She asked.

"I guess there is only one way to find out and that is for you to go with me." He stated. She smiled.

They walked towards the banquet area of the festival when the time came. Their hands kept brushing against each others and finally Max just took her hand in his and played with her thumb once in a while. They seemed to fit together quite nicely. The banquet was in full swing when they got there with another band playing some children's songs until Max's band arrived. Arrive, they did. When David saw who was sitting next to Max at their reserved table, he gave a two thumbs up sign and grinned. Both Max and Abigail grinned back. Max whispered something in

Abigail's ear and she blushed and smiled, then nodded her head. Max beamed back at her and climbed up onto the stage where he picked up his guitar to play.

"My dear brothers and sisters, I wrote a song a few months ago and didn't think I would play it tonight. Well, I would like to announce to you all that...well, my prayers have been answered." He sang the following...

When I find my true love, I will know her

Since I've asked for her in my prayer

Jehovah has shown me what is true love

So I've looked for his guidance from above

She reflects Jehovah's kindness

She reflects Jehovah's peace

She reflects Jehovah's mildness

And she'll see the same in me.

When I find my true love, I will know her

And then we will join our hands together

A three-cord strength, together we'll be bound

For no greater love will there be found

She reflects Jehovah's kindness

She reflects Jehovah's peace

She reflects Jehovah's mildness

And she'll see the same in me.

The applause was thunderous when he ended with the last note.

***

Max had managed to find someone to replace him on guitar so he could dance with Abigail for the rest of the evening. They swept around the floor to the waltz while the band played some new songs as well as the old classics. The dancing got more enthusiastic as the evening wore on and the floor became crowded with many people sharing in the fun. As the floor became more crowded, Max spun Abigail towards the edge of the dance floor and motioned he would get them both something to drink. As he walked away, Abigail's Aunt, Gail drifted closer to her.

"So, my dear, you look very happy. Is this what we think it is?" asked Gail. "Will we be planning a wedding some time in the future?"

"Will you stop!" laughed Abigail. "I just met him today and although we have loved our time together, I'm not presumptuous enough to think it to be more than just two people of similar tastes meeting. We could be on the pathway to a beautiful friendship."

"The pathway down the aisle, you mean." quipped Gail.

"What aisle?" said Gail's brother Joe, walking up with Violet's hand nestled snugly in his.

"Don't listen to her, Uncle Joe, she is having some fun at my expense." replied Abigail.

"Well in that case, since you are paying, what can I do to get in on this kind of deal?" Joe laughed. The others laughed as well but all subsided when Max approached with their drinks. Handing Abigail her drink, he apologized for not getting the others anything. It was fine, they said in unison and just stood there grinning at him.

"What? Did I miss something?" He queried.

"No, you missed nothing at all except family business. Funny business." Abigail silently pleaded with them to cool it and they all gave her minimal nods of the head in ascent.

"Actually, Max, I was wondering if you could do us a big favor?" Said Joe.

"Sure thing, be glad to." he responded.

"Well, Abigail's vacation time is up and she goes back to work tomorrow. We would like her to come stay with us tonight to look over the drawings of the new reception building for those returning in the next round of resurrected ones. If it is possible, could you take her cart home and drop it off at her place as you go home tonight?"

A little disappointed that he wouldn't be able to see her home, Max nevertheless agreed to do so and the subject moved to another area.

"Abigail, I'm afraid I don't know what job you do here. Is it connected to the construction group?" Max asked.

"I'm a New World Life Coach."

"Wait a minute. Abigail...of course! You welcomed back my father last summer. Maxwell Winters?"

" But of course! That is why your name sounds so familiar. You must be his son he was so anxious to greet."

"Guilty. My Dad spoke so highly of you and now I understand why."

"I'm flattered. Your father was a delight to show around. He's part of the reason we are creating a reception building for newly resurrected ones, you know. He mentioned a neutral setting similar to the era the person was living in when they died would make the transition back to the living much easier. They set upon that project right away and now here we are today. Finalizing the plans. " she stated.

"Yes, but taking you away from me tonight. I will be inconsolable." Max feigned hurt.

Abigail laughed, gave him directions to her house and said she was sure he would survive. Thanking him with a hug and hand grip, she climbed into her uncle's carriage. Blowing him a kiss goodnight, she settled back into the seat to reflect on the most wonderful evening she's spent since the new world began.

Chapter Twelve

Joe pulled the carriage into the stable area and jumped down to help the women out. Always the gentleman, he prided himself on being prompt with his assistance and the two women were out and off to the house to prepare for their meeting.

The design of the new building was very important to the resurrection project and Abigail had the most experience of anyone in their area as she received the most people back and had their feedback to go on. Her input had helped them understand the design needed to be one of the nineteenth century as that was the next time frame being resurrected. They had calculated, roughly, the number of people who would be resurrected by using the old census account found in records and also by mathematical equations. It wasn't exact, but it was close enough. There was plenty of land available for the approximate nine billion returning as when Armageddon was over, massive amounts of sea water was drawn from the oceans depths to create a new expanse of water in the heavens where the old one had been prior to the flood. This left a lot of land mass for habitation. It would be rich soil, also as their God was blessing the earth once again. Land masses reconnecting the continents made it easy to go from one continent to the other because, well, there were no more continents. Land connected everywhere. There were new, small islands still off the coast but they were inhabited by animals, for the most part. Visiting them was a delight for a picnic or fun.

Morning dawned to find the three of them hovered over the drawings as more people on the building committee showed up for the coordinating efforts needed for the next round of resurrected ones returning. There were two more weeks in this season and Abigail would be training Josie during those two weeks as she would be taking over part of the returning ones. The nineteenth century resurrected ones would be interesting to meet, that was for sure but it meant spending a little more time with each as there would be more explanations due upon their return.

Most resurrected ones had chosen to stay in the area around where they had lived. David and his long-time friend, Jonathan had decided to travel and ended up locally with Abigail and her family. David had discovered Abigail to be his descendant. Abigail's parents had, in course of time, moved to Roman territory to welcome back more of their ancestry when their time arrived.

David and Jonathan were now among the many who entered Joe's home to determine how the return of the next five hundred years worth of dead would be handled. Abigail had given her input and was ready to go home. Gathering some bags of seed her aunt and uncle had given her, she went out to the horse that was waiting at the porch. He was wearing a light saddle pad and a soft rope halter for guidance purposes, which Abigail would remove when she got home as she would send him off to graze.

He would eventually head back to her Uncle Joe's house as he seemed to really like Joe. The animals chose the people in this new world instead of the other way around. She, herself had several lemurs, two horses, three goats and a chimp who adored her and whom she found hanging around her door when she would step out in the mornings for their greetings from her. She just loved the way the world worked in this new system and looked forward to the centuries ahead. Even more so now that she had met Max last night.

Her thoughts took her back over their meeting and the evenings delights with Max. She felt sure there was something between them and his lovely song kept slipping into her mind. She hummed it now as she decided to walk the three miles to his house to thank him for bringing her equipment back with him last night. As she strolled along with her sandals swinging in her hand, she saw many small animals scurrying along the creek she followed. Rocks, which had been unearthed by the global earthquake that had accompanied Armageddon and the rising of the expanse of water above the earth, now littered the sandy area along the eastern coast. She loved climbing over them to search out small reptiles when younger. Hearing laughter above her, she turned to see several maglevs just above the tree tops moving away from the area of Max's home and so she picked up her pace to see what was going on. Her approach to the house was quiet as she was barefoot, so no one heard her come up his steps to his front door.

She heard Max's voice and hesitated before knocking.

"But I need to go!" she overheard Max saying from an interior room. She started to knock but paused in her knocking. "I love her very much and we need to be together to welcome back our baby...Ouch! My toe! My toe!"

Abigail gasped a slight gasp and turned to lean back against the side of his house. She hadn't meant to eavesdrop and sorely wished she hadn't overheard what she did. She then heard a man's voice respond, though not hearing it well enough to comprehend what was said when Max spoke again.

"Yes, please go to Abigail and explain my short absence to her. She will understand."

But Abigail did not understand and rushed down the steps toward her own home with tears of heartache running down her cheeks. How could she have been so foolish as to think she would have a future with Max? Had he just been polite to someone who was a relative of one of his band member's? What could he have said that made her think he liked her especially? His song? What if she had assumed it was for her but was really for this woman who was the mother of his child that had died in the old system but now being resurrected to them? Why weren't they together?

The pain in her heart gave her feet wings as she ran past her beloved rocks, unseen this time around. She raced up her steps and grabbed several items of clothing to last her a few weeks, tossed them into a satchel and ran out to saddle her own Arabian horse she befriended. She would go stay with Josie to help heal from this heartbreak and wrap herself up in the resurrection work that lay before them.

Chapter Thirteen

The resurrection was proceeding according to the plan laid out by the Faithful and Discreet Slave Class initially and the Presiding Committee now. It was all very organized and amazing as to how it was accomplished. Through Holy Spirit, word was issued forth as to who would be resurrected and where. Coaches were assigned to each new arrival and all their information was gathered and waiting for them when they were brought back. The next of kin who was living was notified so that they could come greet the one brought back and a week of rest and relaxation was given to them as an adjustment period. Very rarely did someone get resurrected in which no one was waiting to greet them. Sometimes it may have been a close friend if parents were not back as yet or they didn't have children. It was very successful as can be imagined. The happiest day of one's life would be to receive a visitor from the Committee stating that someone they loved would return.

Ella sat reading when she heard the gravel crunch in her pathway to her house. Looking up she saw Clark approaching her with a grin. She raised her eyebrows and could only speculate as to why he was grinning. They had met a couple more times over plants and ostriches and had become very close. Perhaps that is why he is grinning, she thought. She had grown to love him very much and yet she wanted to protect her heart from pain so she kept her feelings close and private. Clark felt the same way as she but neither realized it. It didn't prevent them from becoming firm and fast friends, however, which is why Clark was so happy he was bringing the kind of news to Ella that she would love to hear.

"Hello Clark." Said Ella as she greeted him with the hug he always looked forward to receiving from her. "What brings you here this glorious morning?"

"Ah, good news I assure you. Were you aware that I volunteer at the Presiding Committee meetings and am an emissary for them?" He asked.

"Oh, no I didn't know that. Well that must be fun." She stated.

"It can be. Especially if one has good news to share."

"They do the resurrection work, don't they?" She asked.

"Yes they do. Ella, that is why I am here this morning. I have some very good news for you today." He waited for this information to be absorbed before continuing. "I wanted to be the one to let you know that you are to go to the Resurrection Temple tomorrow morning to receive your son back."

Ella paused in organizing the books on her table and clutched one of the publications tightly in her hands. So tightly did she clutch it that her knuckles turned white. She closed her eyes and turned her head towards the sky where she kept thanking Jehovah over and over. A warm arm came around her and pulled her close. She turned in to Clark's arms and burst into tears of joy. The day was finally here. She would see Brian again and be able to raise him in this wonderful new world. She was overjoyed beyond belief. It just seemed to take so long even though time went by so quickly since Armageddon. She had known there would be a great deal of work to be done prior to the resurrection starting. After all, the whole earth had to be brought under paradisaical conditions before the resurrection could begin. Jesus' promise that the evildoer would be with him in Paradise meant just that. The earth had to become a paradise. Now it was a paradise and Brian was returning to her tomorrow. She suddenly felt that she wasn't quite ready. Had she remembered him accurately? He wouldn't realize how long he had been dead as he would think he was waking up from a nap but she had been waiting one hundred forty years for this moment. Her youth had returned and her health was perfect. She was twenty-four when he died and she looked twenty-four now so that wasn't an issue for him. She was so happy! As she held onto Clark, she suddenly felt him grow tense. Something was changing. She paused in her thoughts and tears and looked up at him. He stared down at her and used his fingertip to dry the tears from her cheek. Then he slowly lowered his head and gently kissed her lips with such warmth and love that the tears began for her again.

"Don't cry, Ella. I'm sorry. I shouldn't have kissed you. It is just that I know how happy you are and how this must be wrenching at your heart." He claimed.

"No…no, don't apologize at all. I'm very happy. You've made me happy twice in one fell swoop. First with news of Brian and then a kiss to rival all kisses. Thank you so very much for this wonderful day."

"Oh, Ella, you don't know how long I have wanted to kiss you. I love you so very much and I know my timing may be off but I would like us to be a family. I want to share tomorrow with you so much. Please, will you let me share this time with you and will you promise to become my wife?" He asked her.

"Yes. Plain and simple. Yes, yes, yes. I've loved you for years and years. I just didn't know it until I met you in person. The first phase of my love was fantasy and idealistic. This second phase of my love is from the bottom of my heart for a man who loves Jehovah as much as I and who shares my interests and loves. Yes, yes, yes. I will promise to you all that you want. I love you so much."

They spent the rest of the day planning their future and when Clark left for home, Ella collapsed upon her bed thinking she would not be able to sleep due to anxiety for tomorrow. Exhaustion overtook her. The next thing she knew, it was morning. Clark was calling up to her from below and the sunlight was blazing in through a break in the leaves. Ella jumped up and changed her clothes after a brisk wash down. She lighted down next to Clark and hand in hand they headed for his cart.

137

Their arrival was perfect timing. Max and Angie came to greet their brother. They were ushered in to a room with a bed surrounded by drawn drapes, similar to a hospital room. Ella came to a halt in front of the life coach, Susan, standing by the bed.

"Are you ready Ella?" Asked Susan. Ella could only nod.

"Then Ella, may I present you with your son, Brian." She pulled back the curtain and Brian was sitting there in a small hospital type gown. He grinned when he saw his mother and he hopped off the bed to run towards her. He threw his arms around her.

"Mommy! Give me a big ole hug."

* * *

The days went by rapidly for Abigail as she went through the training session for Josie, who lived just off the beach close to Claudia's home. Claudia had heard of Abigail's arrival and decided to invite herself to join them and become a life coach herself. It was becoming more fun for Abigail as, each day that distanced her from her heartache, was welcomed. Josie and Claudia were unaware of Abigail's plight because she had chosen not to reveal it to them, thus sparing herself the additional pain of rehashing the hurt. Days were spent in training and nights were spent reading about the era of the nineteenth century. It would only take a decade to bring back those who had died in the southern region and teach them. Then it would be on to the eighteenth century, seventeenth century and so on until they got to where the Native American Indians would return. That meant a whole new set of coaches and their jobs were over. A life settled in one area to call home. Home. The word brought tears to her eyes, which she wiped away before anyone noticed.

"Okay, we've been at this nonstop for over a week now and I think our brains need a break." declared Josie as she stretched her arms high over her head; twisting first to the left, then right.

"I agree." said Claudia. "Having been one to have been resurrected, I can tell you know what you are doing and we are way ahead of the game so its break time." she announced. "Who wants to go surfing?" Cheers went up all around and the girls changed into shorts and t-shirts to head for the beach.

Josie had several boards to choose from and each girl grabbed their board of choice and strolled down to where many people had already gathered with their friends or family. Several lions strolled the beach and dogs dashed in and out, around them, playfully. Squirrel monkeys swung from the trees where beautiful parrots and a cock-a-too or two perched. The palm branches gave evidence of a breeze as they swayed, creating an interesting pattern in the sand below them. The girls found a shady spot where they could lay their towels and blankets and took off with their boards to the beach.

The waves were not the best but that suited them just fine. The just wanted a change of pace, not fight strong waves. After about a half hour of riding waves and shared laughter over mishaps in the water, they decided to come ashore. Leaning the boards against the palm trees, they lay down, exhausted beneath the tree.

"You girls look like you're having fun." They heard a voice say.

"Mom!" exclaimed Claudia. "How nice to see you!" She jumped up to give her mom a hug. Her mother, Cheryl, was surrounded by six small children. "Did you bring your class on a field trip today?" she asked.

"Yes, I did. I am teaching them today about focusing. They need to be able to levitate sooner than later so I thought a field trip would be a good proving ground, so to speak, with less damage to the rump should they drop themselves." she laughed.

"Good point! You can't beat sand for cushioning the blow. What will you use?"

"Coconuts." She pointed up to where several coconuts hung above their heads. The small children looked up and squealed with delight.

"This we've got to see." exclaimed Claudia as she sat back down next to Abigail and Josie.

The six children gathered around Cheryl as she started to explain the fundamentals of faith in yourself and God. She then demonstrated her own ability to levitate up to the coconut and touched it. She then held one of the children's hand and helped them levitate to touch the coconut. In turn, they each practiced. Then it was time for them to try it alone. With many false starts and many bruised bottoms later, they all finally managed to levitate up to touch a coconut. Squeals of delight while jumping up and down drew the attention of others who smiled and waved their congratulations to the small boys and girls. Cheryl then collected them together and hugging her daughter goodbye, set off towards the day care center she managed, with her sister, Sheilah. Parents most often taught their own young but when both were off for the day working on a construction site somewhere, they loved having the option of a day working together without fear of children under foot getting hurt or disrupting the job.

Claudia watched her mother walk away with six children in tow and sighed.

"What's the sigh for?" asked Josie.

'Oh, I don't know. Seeing Mom with all those children, I guess. She would make a wonderful mother, don't you think?" she asked wistfully.

"Well, she sure did a good job with you. Why doesn't she sign up for foster care?" asked Abigail.

"What do you mean?"

"I mean she should sign up for the Foster Care Program we start next month for the last few weeks of this resurrection cycle. You know, where the babies who were lost during pregnancy would be brought back to life but their parents didn't make it through Armageddon?" Explained Abigail.

"What! This is the first I'm hearing of it."

"Yeah, me too! What are you saying?" asked Josie.

"Well don't you remember the song my Grand Uncle David wrote about in the Bible? It went like this: 'Your eyes saw even the embryo of me, And in your book all its parts were down in writing?' Well, why wouldn't a loving god bring back to life all those whose loving personality, traits and whose DNA was known to Him? They have a right to life and in reading their tiny hearts, he knows who they will become. See?"

Claudia sat thinking for a few minutes, then tears slowly rolled down her cheeks. Confused as to why, they questioned her in earnest.

"My mother lost a baby boy before she had me! Oh, this will make her so happy to hear. I have to go tell her this news. But, yes, you are right about her becoming a foster mother. She would love that. Catch ya later." she called out as she jumped up from the sand to take off after her mother and her children entourage.

"Well that is certainly good news. I bet Max's mother will feel doubly blessed. She lost a little girl she was carrying about two years after Max was born. The reason she decided to have Max was because she had already lost one son, aged three, born

142

before him. Hey, that reminds me! How did that go? I heard her little boy was resurrected the day after the festival. Angie and Max must have been so excited. Did they rush to their mother's side to be there for her?"

Abigail's color began to fade as the truth about the situation with Max began to penetrate her brain. It was his brother returning, not his son! And the one he loved must have been his sister! Slow dread at what he must be thinking or doing now began to seep in and it was becoming too much. Her guilt at eavesdropping and not waiting for an explanation was starting to weigh heavy on her heart. She burst into tears of regret and sorrow.

Josie was struck with perplexity. Not knowing what was wrong or what to do, she did what any friend would do. She wrapped her arms around Abigail and let her cry it out. After about ten minutes of sniffles and nose blowing, Abigail raised her head and looked into Josie's eyes.

"I'm an idiot." she stated simply.

"Oh, well, that would make me cry, too." grinned Josie. Abigail's laugh burst forth but quickly turned to tears again. She finally got control of herself to explain what had transpired that day as Josie shook her head while still encouraging her to complete her story. When she was finished, Josie simply said that she was

143

right, she was an idiot. Abigail gave her a halfhearted punch.

"Wow, girl. Did it not occur to you that he would explain if you had made yourself known? I mean, he did say you would understand, right?" she asked.

"Will you please try to remember that we only met the day before and that I hardly know him?"

"Yes, but Abigail, we are no longer living in that world where duplicity ruled. He would have told you right away if he had a past relationship with someone that included a child."

"Well, of course he would have. I just never thought I would be so fortunate as to find someone so loving as he. What must he think of me, now? What can I do to rectify this situation I have created?" She asked.

"I'm not sure, but I would be honest with him. He will understand, I feel sure."

Nodding her head, Abigail arose from the sand and started back towards Josie's house with Josie keeping a modest pace behind knowing Abigail needed to think.

The next morning, Abigail had her horse packed up and ready to return to her own house and see what kind of repair job she could do to fix this mess she had made. She had said her good-byes to Josie and was no more than fifty feet away when Josie called her to come back, waving a large piece of paper in her hand.

Running towards Abigail, who had turned her horse and headed back, she was a bit winded when they met.

"Here, this is for you. The messenger was at the front door while you were going out the back. It looks very important and official." explained Josie. Abigail took it to read.

"They are asking me to come to what used to be Atlanta to help with the resurrection there. It is further behind than we are because there was so much more cleanup work to do. They need me to help for just a short time, training some, coaching some. Well, how am I to get there? This is too far to travel at the speed they need me there for this horse." explained Abigail.

"I think that is why the messenger is still here. He is probably your ride there and back."

This was indeed the case, as he waited outside Josie's front door on his dual passenger maglev vehicle. He introduced himself as Lars and helped Abigail stow her bag behind the back brace of her seat. She hugged Josie and said the note told her it would only be for two weeks. Climbing on, she situated herself behind Lars and waved good-bye as they rose into the air.

"Look after my horse till I get back?"

Josie nodded her agreement as she watched the two pick up speed and zoom off towards the west. That was a six hour trip she did not envy them.

Chapter Fourteen

Area previously known as Atlanta

The meeting had ended a half an hour ago and everyone was standing around outside the arena that was starting to bloom with the sweet fragrance of wisteria, which hung in grape-like clusters from the columns. The sun was starting to go down behind the mighty oaks that surrounded the arena, casting parts of the columns in dappled shade while allowing the sun to catch a sparkle or two from the marbled construction. The excited chatter among the visitors was louder than the usual din because a momentous announcement had just been made.

"May I have your attention, please?" Came a loud call from the podium at the center of the amphitheater type arena. All present stopped talking and turned their attention to the speaker.

"Please come closer for just a few minutes more as I repeat some instructions which have actually changed just a little. We told you to list your current family members so you can receive adjacent property but what we forgot to tell you is that you need to include any family members who are awaiting the resurrection because guess what?"

An anxious hush fell over the crowd and all present moved as one to get closer to the speaker. Looks passed between many there as speculation grew. Could it be?

"I know the restoration progress in other areas has been faster than here and many have seen their loved ones return already. I am pleased to announce that we have been guided to inform you that children you lost in death in the old system will start returning within a month from today! What do you think of that, my friends?"

A jubilant, thundering roar rose from the crowd as many applauded and shouted and men hugged their wives while shifting between tears and laughter at the good news. Congratulatory hugs and slaps on the back were just part of the commotion as families lined up at the tables set up for registry.

"Here you go, sign here and include family names here and ages here." Said the brother behind the table as he presented the clipboard to the first person in line. There were at least twenty assistants behind that many tables so as to speed up the process of registering. Private instructions were given to each family head depending on their circumstances and disposition. But all were told to expect notification within the month as to where their property would be located. Some had actually received their land ahead of schedule due to their work assignment of growing the vegetables and fruits for consumption by the cleaners of the earth. Helen was one of those. There was plenty to do.

As the registration came to a close, the elders who collected the census gathered to meet back at the arena stage. A large round table had been set up with twenty chairs around it. This was going to be a huge task and they needed to meet to see how they would proceed. A huge map of the area was in the center of the table along with stickpins. Large candles had been strategically placed so as to afford enough light as the evening wore on past nightfall. The elders had thought that each couple would receive about three acres and had made that announcement several years ago but through thorough investigation and help from the holy spirit, it was determined that many people liked living in mountainous areas while others preferred the beach. While this would have been a problem in the old system due to irrigation issues, in this wonderful new world it was not a problem at all. Jehovah had blessed the land and now each family head would receive five acres plus adjacent five acre plots each for their children still at home. No one would be forced to remain in the same place for eternity but this would make a nice start. What would happen during the resurrection would be completely in Jesus' hands along with his Princes'.

This process went on for a few hours and just as promised, the assignments had been completed and sent out by courier to each temporary dwelling home. There were plenty of single parents who would be receiving their resurrected children back soon and they were given special attention so as to accommodate their needs. What they had not shared with anyone as yet was the news that many who had lost a child prior to birth would be receiving them back also. It was something unclear prior to Armageddon but had recently come to a full understanding through Holy Spirit and prayer. Instructions were now included in each packet that let them know when they would be receiving an extra five acres due to a miscarried child's new chance through the resurrection. They wanted to let that be something learned in the privacy of their own home where emotions would no doubt run high. It was wonderful news and each brother in that arena had a glorious countenance from sheer happiness at being given the privilege of sharing that good news.

Helen was one of the single sisters who had lost a child during the pregnancy and who's husband had divorced her to marry another woman. They had not survived the battle but Helen did. She was happy to get her five acres and waited patiently to see where it would be located. She loved the mountains and hoped she would have land somewhere close to them. She had learned what kind of plants grew in shady areas and planned to clear out a portion for a vegetable garden in a sunny location. She had picked up her allotment of fruit trees from the communal nursery so she would have some sort of decent start of her garden. She knew that some fruit trees needed another one for pollination so she did have duplicates of some. All in all, she had a count of fifteen trees and of course, two were fig trees. She loaded them all in the back of her wagon. She had a wagon, which resembled the buckboards of the old West in the old system. There were improvements, of course, but the horsepower remained the same, two. Her two Morgan horses were sturdy for the trip up the mountain and she could also use them for plowing later. She climbed up onto the seat of her wagon and was about to start out on her lonely journey towards the mountain named Mount Camel for its two hump-like rises when a young brother ran up to her to prevent her departure.

"My sister, Helen! You are wanted at the registration office quickly." He panted.

"Oh my! You look exhausted. You must have run the whole two miles. It must be important, huh?"

"I'm not sure but I would say a big 'yes' to that." He grinned. "They had tried to catch you before you left but you got away through the crowd and so they sent me. Whew! Can I hitch a ride back with you?"

"Of course you can, silly. Did you think I would make you walk?" She laughed. Deep down inside, however, she was curious beyond all belief. What did the registrars have in need for her, she pondered? I guess I'm about to find out, she thought as she pulled up in front of the registrar's office building.

There were people milling about inside the foyer, which looked like a grand hotel lobby. They all looked very happy and so many of them had backpacks stuffed with seed packets and small tools for gardening. They kept hugging each other and wishing each other much success and because it was such a happy sight, it brought tears of joy to Helen's eyes. The tears were what the registrar saw when she walked into his office a few minutes later.

"Oh, did someone tell you already?" he asked?

"Tell me what?" Helen inquired nervously.

"Never mind. I saw the tears and thought you had been given the good news already."

"OK, now I am too curious. I'm glad you said it is good news but why would my tears of joy from seeing my friends out there so happy be misconstrued that I have already received good news from here?"

"Well, because we have some good news, that is all. However, I need some assistance in sharing this news so I will ask our Life Coach to come in for this. Abigail, can you come in here for a few minutes?" He called into the adjacent room.

"What's up?" Abigail asked as she walked into the room.

"This is Helen that we sent for earlier. I thought it would be nice if she had a sister here with her, don't you think?" He asked.

"Oh, of course. That is my job. Plus, you know me, I love to be present when such good news goes forth." She grinned.

"Well, you have me totally curious and a little anxious. What news do you have for me?" asked Helen.

"Please have a seat and Abigail, sit next to her there." Phil, the registrar said as he moved to sit behind his own desk. "Helen, we have received direction from the Faithful and Discreet Slave that it has been determined that those women who lost a child

151

while pregnant would be given the opportunity to complete that pregnancy and to give birth. We understand you lost a son quite early on in your pregnancy?"

Helen went numb. First, because she would be given the wonderful blessing of having a child and second because she hadn't known what sex the baby had been. Her mind began doing strange things like going numb and then racing in all directions and then shutting down and starting up again. It was just too much to take in all of a sudden. She simply rested her face into her hands and wept. She wept for a very long time and Abigail rubbed her back while she wept. Both Phil and Abigail had tears of joy in their eyes for their sister who had suffered such a great loss at one time but whom Jehovah would now bless for her loyalty.

At last the tears gave way to a glorious and peaceful smile as Helen raised her head high and wiped away the last of the tears. She stood and hugged them both and then asked;

"How does this all work, do you know?"

"Yes. Holy spirit will come upon you tonight while you sleep. You will not be able to tell at first because you lost him early. Some of our sisters lost their baby just before birth and it has been quite an experience for them to suddenly be filled with a full term baby, believe me. But the process must be completed within you so as to develop that oneness you will share with your baby at birth. You may want to let your neighboring sisters know so that they can assist you at that time but delivery will be easy now that women no longer carry that curse of painful delivery." Phil answered.

"A son. I am to have a son. I shall name him Patrick after my father."

"Yes, your father is slated to return himself shortly, followed the next month by your mother so I understand."

"Yes, indeed. I got the news last week and was thrilled. But this news thrills me beyond all that and that was a lot. How can we not be bursting with joy at all this good news? I have never known such joy in my whole life and I owe it all to Jehovah."

"We all owe Jehovah so much. My parents returned two weeks ago and we are thrilled. Now, my sister, if you will step through this door here, we will adjust your portion of land to accommodate one more." Phil opened a side door and escorted her into another vast room with record keeping capabilities. The rest of the afternoon was a blur to Helen but she made it through and went out into the brilliant sunshine to climb back onto her wagon once more. She noticed a few additions to her load which would accommodate another mouth to feed and with her paperwork tucked neatly in her dress pocket, she slapped the reins to head her wagon back out towards Mount Camel and her acreage.

The ride up the mountain was such a beautiful sight to Helen. When the group, which signed up for mountain living, had been selected for this mountain, they had all explored it with great anticipation. It offered something for all their needs. A brook trickled down from the very top where a spring created an overflow. The other mountainous hump had a stream, likewise. Both water sources supplied anyone's needs for water on the mountain. Beautiful flowers could be gathered from the stream's banks for beautifying one's home. She stopped to gather some before heading around the bend to her home. Her home had been one of the new designed quick-build types that could be added to at any time should one's family increase. Her own family was about to increase by one. Wait, she corrected. No, now I have a family whereas before it was just I. So, now I will get to add on a room for Patrick, she thought. She moved her hand to her abdomen to feel it empty still. She would be pregnant by tomorrow morning was the promise. She looked forward to it in great anticipation and was excited to share the news with others once it happened. For now, she would be happy to just get her supplies put away and get some much needed rest from all the excitement this day had brought. She placed her bouquet in a vase on the table and prepared herself a small meal.

As the night bore on, Helen focused on what she needed to accomplish tomorrow with the planting of her trees and laying out her garden. Her grocery supply would last her two weeks before she would have to go back to replenish her pantry. She could stretch it to three weeks if she made a large pot of soup with some of it. She would like to cut back on going to the village much if she were to get much done here. She paused as she thought of her

154

grocery list. She smiled as she suddenly realized that she would now be eating for two and needed to adjust her list accordingly. Tears arrived unexpectedly to her eyes as pure happiness began to overflow her heart. Sleep finally overtook her as well as exhaustion and she closed her eyes.

The sun began to rise just as Helen began to awaken. She rolled over in her bed to move open the curtain to let in the sunlight and to let her see it rising. She stretched and rolled over to her back when she suddenly remembered that this morning would be the morning of major changes in her body. She lay still for a few minutes and then rested her hand on her tummy. She felt just a slight rise in her tummy region but that was all. She didn't feel much different. Maybe it didn't work. She suddenly felt something move inside her and her joy knew no bounds. She placed both her hands on her tummy and waited for the next movements. That was what she was doing when she heard a knock on her door.

Jumping up, she grabbed her housecoat to put on prior to opening the door. When she opened the door, she looked up into the most beautiful brown eyes she had ever seen. The brother before her was tall and tanned and, yes, quite lovely to look upon. Helen felt warmth growing all through her body as she felt his gaze upon her grow with interest.

"Good morning, my brother, may I help you?"

He grinned. Then he grinned again.

"I should introduce myself. My name is Phillip Laws and I am you new neighbor."

"Oh, well, excellent. Welcome to Mount Camel." Helen mumbled in confusion. "What can I do for you?" She asked again.

"Well, actually my sister, it is more like what I can do for you." He stated.

"What do you mean?" Helen asked with much anticipation as her breath was just now returning. "What can you do for me?"

"You didn't expect Jehovah to make you raise your son alone, did you? I do believe we have a child to raise together. I know you were not expecting me and that there is a lot to explain so perhaps we can sit out here in the sunshine and have ourselves a nice long chat."

Helen nodded numbly and sat down on a chair under her outdoor umbrella.

***

Abigail had been here two weeks and this was her last assignment. She was ready to go home and face the music with Max. Would Max forgive her?

Chapter Fifteen

Abigail was dropped off at her place by Lars and she waved her farewells as he sped back to his home. She was so glad to be back in her own bed at last. The last month since the festival had been both exciting and turbulent as she dwelt on how she would face Max. If he even wanted to see her again. The thought that he might not want to see her had her pacing the floor. 'I mean, I took off without telling him I was leaving or anything.' She thought. 'How will I be able to justify my actions?'

She went ahead and prepared herself for bed. Climbing under the sheets to draw them up around her, she pulled her long hair out of its clip to brush it out before braiding it for the night. One hundred strokes was what her grandmother had told her to do. Every night you must brush your hair one hundred strokes, she would say, to get the circulation going. Her hair was just past her waist and curly and she would trim it back to that length as anything longer would just get in her way and became too much for her job. She barely had time to grow her lovely flowers she sold at each quarterly festival let alone coach resurrected ones to have time to mess with extra long hair. Tossing her hair over her shoulder after braiding it, she snuggled herself down and fell fast asleep.

The sun coming through her window woke her up the next

morning. She could hear the sound of something stepping around on her porch and she suspected her animals had discovered she had returned. She would be glad to see her little goats and lovely Arabian. She threw back her covers and climbed out of bed. Grabbing a long cotton, pink robe, she slipped it on to go to her kitchen in order to fix herself a cup of tea. She had grown tea bushes and in the spring had harvested and dried them for just such a time of the morning. The air was a little cooler now that fall was late upon them and even though it would never again be so bitterly cold in winter, it still would be cool enough to add layers before going outside. But today was just lovely, she noticed as she looked out her kitchen window. It faced her herb garden and the sun, in the east, as that is how she planned it when they came to build her house so many years ago.

With most of the kitchen facing the north, she had planned her home so that her bedroom and one wall of her kitchen faced the rising sun. She loved watching it in the morning so she grabbed her tea and walked out the kitchen door to walk around the wrapped porch to the east side where she could continue to watch the sun rise. The air smelled of sweet honeysuckle and roses. Birds of nearly every variety sat in trees to sing their morning songs. A distant dog barking told her her neighbors were waking up whether they wanted to or not. She grinned to herself. Her little world was waking up and everything was beautiful. And then she remembered her quest for today. To go see Max and apologize. She decided to practice what she would say while she prepared her breakfast of bread and cheese and fruit. Her cold cellar had kept things nice and fresh while she was away so there was plenty to eat before she needed to prepare more.

They had told her that she should take some time off after her trip so that she could settle back into her local routine. She had learned a great deal while in old Atlanta and planned to utilize it once she got rested and refreshed. It wouldn't take that long, after all she was drawing nearer the perfection Adam had lost to them and therefore her body would recuperate faster. She paused long enough to wrap her long hair into a top knot while fixing her meal so it wouldn't get in her way. Picking up her tray, she took it to the porch once more so she could view her garden to determine what needed to be done once she returned from seeing Max.

The lilac bushes still held a few stray clusters of blossoms, which delighted her tremendously as that was her favorite flower. As she munched on the bread, she saw the need to pinch off some rose buds. The kale was growing tall which meant it was time for her to harvest that. She liked roasting it in her oven with some olive oil and garlic. Then there was the pumpkins she needed to lift off the ground before they rotted on the bottom. The gourds were just about ready to pluck off the vine and dry. She hoped she had some interesting shapes this year as she wanted to make some unique bird houses out of them.

So lost in though was she that she didn't hear the horse

gallop up until it was at her front porch. Recognizing Max, Abigail set her breakfast aside to get ready for her confrontation with him. She brushed the crumbs off her shirt and smoothed hack the sides of her hair of any flyaway strands. He came barreling around the corner of her porch with purposeful strides and grabbed her hands with both of his.

"Please tell me you will forgive my absense this past month. Your uncle just told me he didn't get to speak with you to tell you of my sudden departure. I had hoped he would so you wouldn't worry about why I haven't called on you. Now, well, I am begging you to forgive me, my dear Abigail and let me back into your good graces." he said with such tender earnestness. Totally bewildered by the turn of events, Abigail could only stare with her mouth open. Seeing her this way, he felt she might be on the edge of forgiving him so he dropped down on one knee and said he would never smile again if she didn't forgive him.

That is when the irony of the situation hit her and her smile turned from whimsey to chuckles to laughter. She had to sit down. This was too much. All this time, they were both worried about something the other one knew nothing about. She laughed till her side started to hurt. Max didn't see the humor yet as she hadn't shared her part yet but when she finally got her part of the deed out, he sat down and joined her in laughter.

"So we aren't mad at each other and we promise to trust each other to be open and careful with each others feelings in the future. Right?" Max queried.

"I have no problem with that at all. So, tell me about your trip and I will tell you mine."

They sat for hours on her porch telling and retelling parts that were funny and just generally enjoying each others company. They got up to walk around in her garden. Abigail opened her decorative mailbox from of old to withdraw a sharp pocket knife. She walked over to where the sunflowers were growing well over fifteen feet high. She worked her hand up the stalk and then bent it down to cut the flower off six inches down from it. She repeated this with several others.

"Wouldn't you want the stems a bit longer for your bouquet?" Max asked.

"Mmm, if this were for a bouquet. But I need to dry these so I can use the seeds for birds, my snacks and next years crop." she smiled.

"Of course, how silly of me. I just remember how much you love your bouquets of flowers. I would love for you to come see my garden. Its mostly bottle gourds right now but in the spring, there are all sorts of flowers blooming there. I plow a space about ten feet wide by two hundred and leave it sit for a few days and sure enough, before long my sister sneaks in and casts flower seed there by the thousands. She will come just after they start to sneak up through the ground and convinces me that I shouldn't grow any vegetables there. We've been playing this game for ten years now. She probably has figured out that I do it just for her." he smiled thinking of it.

What a delightful man he is, she decided. She was drawing closer to him every hour they spent together. Unfortunately, she didn't have much time left before she had to go back to coaching. Thinking of that she spun around to confront him.

"That reminds me. Were you aware that there is to be a pregnancy renewal time frame starting soon?"

"Not sure what you mean. Explain, please."

"Well, as you know, some women lost children in their early pregnancies and these were embryos Jehovah 'knew'. So, there is a directory in place now for women who lost their children in the womb to receive them either as a newborn if a later loss at seven months or more. Or receive them back in their womb for growth. You know, if he did this with Jesus, he can certainly do it with the rest of us."

"Are you saying my mother may carry my baby sister we lost at four months through to full term?" His mouth slowly opened in an O.

"Yes. I have this list in the house of the first hundred. Shall we go in?"

They went in to her house with Max holding her elbow, ever the gentleman. She liked that. Just knowing he was here with her gave her a warm sense of comfort and peace. She went over to her desk, which was in the far corner of her living room, facing a window for light. She withdrew a sheet of paper from the drawer to unfold it. They were still working on ways to make the pulp thinner when pressing it for paper but for now the pages were still a tad bit thick, like manilla folders. She unfolded it and began reading the list out loud.

"That's her. Right there." he stated excitedly.

"But that is Ella Weller. Your name is Winters."

"Yes, yes, she recently married."

"But I know her! We trade flower seeds each fall. She says she gives half to her daughter who gives half of that to her brother. You are her son who receives my seeds?" Another coincidence that brought chuckles to their lives and yet made them pause.

"Are you thinking what I am thinking?" he asked.

"Depends on what you are thinking."

"I'm thinking someone with much bigger plans for us than we ourselves have is behind these odd coincidences. What do you think?"

"I think you may be right. What do you think we should do about it?" she asked as her gaze lowered to where his lips had just opened slightly to exhale. She saw them come closer and just before they touched her lips, she looked up into his eyes and was lost forever.

The kiss that began as a tentative exploration gradually grew into one of profound glory and love from both of them. At last they pulled away and he enveloped her in his strong arms. His muscles flexed as he started to pick her up but thought better of it as he suddenly let go and instead bent down on one knee. She gasped.

"No, don't be surprised. You must know by now that we fit together so well and it would be a shame to put off uniting ourselves just for propriety sake. I have grown to love you so very much over this last month. You mean more to me than any other person. I want us to become one and serve our God together. Abigail, will you marry me?"

Her head began to nod her ascent before she could catch her breath to speak. At last the words she'd long to say for so long began to reveal her feelings for him.

"Oh my darling, Max, yes, yes I would be most honored to be your wife. You see, I have loved you from first we met. I felt so connected to you from the very beginning but was so afraid to think you could care for me, too. I can think of no one with whom I'd rather spend eternity than you. So, yes, yes, I will marry you." They sealed it with another glorious kiss.

Chapter Sixteen
The Folks

Ella had her baby three weeks before the wedding. Abigail and she had grown quite close in view of the fact that she would soon be Abigail's mother-in-law soon, so she wanted her there when she delivered. Maxwell Sr. was there to greet his daughter and even though their marriage had ended with his death, he wanted to share responsibility for his daughter. It was an unexpected gift and a tremendous blessing from their God. She came out screaming legs and arms flailing. She was beautiful to them all and her blue eyes matched her brothers. Abigail saw that right away and became a little wistful when thinking about having children herself. A tiny tear of joy rolled down her cheek.

"Hey, what's this?" he asked, wiping it away with his thumb while his curled fingers supported her chin. He tilted her chin up to plant a small, affectionate kiss on the end of her nose. "Want one too?" he asked.

"I guess that is something we should talk about, I suppose." she answered.

"Yes and probably before the wedding. How about we get Mom settled in for a few days then we can plan a picnic to discuss it, okay?" She nodded her agreement.

She had a wedding to plan and her two bridesmaids, Josie

and Claudia, were due in at the end of the week to stay with her till the wedding. There was so much to do. Her parents were arriving the day before the wedding as that is how long it would take to get there from Rome. They did not like the maglevs and so would travel by carriage the whole trip. Josie and Claudia would be on hand to help the bride with the arrangements and reception. The wedding would be held in her garden as that would be the last time she would live there. She wanted the memory of their wedding to be from there. They planned to set up housekeeping in Max's home since it was nearly three times larger than hers.

Max had set up a simple archway in the garden at the center circle of Abigail's rose garden. It was in full bloom and the scent was sweet. Chairs would be set up the day of the wedding for the forty or so guests when they arrived. Tables with chairs for the reception afterward would go in the herb garden between two rosemary bushes for the scent. It was just off the kitchen so the food would be easier to serve. It would be a joyous day.

Ten days before the wedding, Max stopped by Abigail's house carrying a picnic basket.

"Would you care to join me for an afternoon of witty conversation and repartee?" he asked, tongue in cheek.

"Sure thing. Know where I could find some?" she grinned. He just growled and grabbed her around the waist to pull her close.

"I warn you woman, I can be witty any time I want. But right now I just want to stare into those beautiful blue eyes of

166

yours."

"I'll settle for that. Are we ready for this picnic talk, you think?" she asked.

"Yeah, I think so." Grabbing her hand in his left one while holding the basket in the other, they set off towards one of the many lakes that had formed inland with the rise of the water to the canopy. Exposing land masses from that had left huge puddles that were considered small lakes to everyone. They were just large enough to sail a tiny skiff around for an hour or two. They all had beaches as that was all there was; sand. But importing dirt helped support the landscaping.

He found a spot about fifty feet from another couple so they were assured some privacy. They pulled out their food and helped themselves to whatever he had brought with him. She had brought a jug of sweet tea and mugs, which they shared. They chatted over small nothings until they finished their lunch and put things away. Then, spreading the blanket further out, he positioned himself so she could sit next to him instead of opposite him and he patted the space next to him for her to sit there.

"I guess we need to discuss our future together and how we will function as a family. I love the sound of that, don't you?" She nodded wordlessly.

"So, to get us started, I think we should remember that we have eternity before us. We have all the time in the world." he said.

"Well, maybe not." she said. He frowned. She continued. "Well, the command was to *fill* the earth and so at some point, it will be filled. How many will be resurrected is an unknown factor." she reminded him.

"Hmm, this is true. But we do have a few years to go, wouldn't you say?" he asked.

"Yes. Look, I want to have you to myself for a few years, if that is what you are wondering." she said.

He grinned and nodded. Giving her hand a gentle squeeze, he drew it up to his lips to kiss it.

"Yes, I want time for more of that." she teased lightly. He laughed and planted a quick kiss on her lips.

"Now, as to how many." he pondered. She let him think for a while and then spoke up.

"Perhaps we should wait to see how the first one goes."

"Nope, you don't get your way on this one. I want nine sons. You can have as many daughters as you want." he waggled his eye brows at her and she laughed.

"Not the old 'I gotta have enough for a baseball team' routine!" she laughed. "Women play baseball as well as you men do." She haughtily turned her nose up into the air.

"Sure you do, only different. So, nine boys and nine girls so you can have your own team, too." he declared. She laughed, fell against his side and put her arms around him, hugging him close.

Knowing they hadn't made much progress except for waiting awhile to have children, they packed it all up and headed back to Abigail's house. Standing there to greet them were her two bridesmaids. Grinning from ear to ear, the two women ushered Max off to his house in short order so that they could get started on the wedding decor plans.

The colors would be a soft lavender with accents of darker purple and the greenery surrounding them. The food choices would be some of her Aunt Violet's blueberry tarts instead of a cake as the old traditions had made way for common sense ideas where waste was not smart. Violet chose her blueberry tarts when she heard Abigail's color choice as, according to her, it stained lavender anyway. So, the time went from a slow crawl of anticipation to a quick 'we don't have enough time' pace.

The time arrived for her parents to get there, so Abigail had prepared her little guest cottage for them, for privacy sake. The girls were camped inside her little house on cots. They loved being together like this to plan, laugh and share jokes about married life. Gathering together some daisies and peonies, her Mom's favorite two flowers, she filled the cottage to the brim in order to make it seem fresh and lovely. She hadn't seen her folks in two years and she was so thrilled that her wedding was what brought them home to her, if only for a few days. Her running to the front door every half hour was beginning to wear everyone out. They said so. She was told that time would go by faster if she kept herself busy doing something besides pacing back and forth to the door. Relenting, she finally went into the kitchen to make a fruit salad. No sooner was she in the kitchen then Josie called out, "They're here!"

Dropping the oranges back into the bowl, she made a mad dash for the front door. They were here! She was so excited to see them that she rushed out the door and down towards the lane where their open carriage came to a halt.

"Mom! Dad! Oh, it is so good to see you!" She tried to embrace them both, failed and then hugged them each twice. "I can hardly believe you are standing here. I'm so happy to see you." at which point, she burst into tears. Hugging her, they smiled at each other over her head as she bent into her mother's arms.

There was so much to be discussed that they decided to put off unpacking until all the news was shared. Abigail told of her meeting with Max and how wonderful he was. Her parents, Thomas and Cora were thrilled that she found someone to love and who loved her in return. They grinned at each other when they thought about the possibility of grandchildren, though she blushed at the idea. She was so happy with all the people in her life so close now. The thought was warming but then the knowledge that they would be leaving so soon after the wedding made her sad, too. But, she had them with her now and she was getting caught up with their activities, also.

"So, what is new with you two?" she asked.

They looked at each other and grinned.

"Well, we are very excited about some recent discoveries in the marine world. As you know, we have been living in what used to be Italy, on an island still called Sardinia. What we discovered when we would row to the mainland, yes row, was that the dolphin population was more than happy to assist us in many things around the island. With Jehovah sucking so much water back up to the heavenly realm, there is not that much distant to the mainland. The island is much bigger now. So, with the creation of more land mass came the creation of new bays and such. Dolphins love bay areas. They came much closer to us and we discovered their desire to help us with dock construction and so forth. They click away at us to let us know they are willing and we figured out that they love to fetch things or deliver things to other builders in the area. If tools are dropped in the bay, they retrieve them. It is all so much fun and they love small children to play with so you can imagine the delight of the children." said Thomas

"Sounds wonderful, Dad. Is the construction of docks your specialty these days?" she asked.

"We both lend a hand where it is needed." he replied.

"Honey, there is so much that has been done in the region. You just wouldn't believe it. We went over to the Roman area a year or so ago and the gardens they have established are just tremendously beautiful. There are plants growing there that we have never seen before! There are so many new creations. It is unbelievable." said Cora

They went on to relate all the things that were happening in that region and shared wonderful experiences they had with animals and people. They all chatted while snacking until the wee hours of the morning. Sleep finally overtook them and Abigail's promise that they would meet Max first thing in the morning put smiles on her parents faces and they went to their room for the night.

Morning brought beautiful sunshine and a lovely breeze with it as Max made his way to Abigail's house to meet her parents. He had heard a lot of amazing stories about how they were pioneers in the dolphin training techniques and he would love to start some sort of program here like theirs. He enjoyed his work with the band and making wooden toys or instruments was great but nature called to him, too. Especially the dolphin community. He hoped they would share. He knew they would, in fact. He was really looking forward to this day. Since all mankind had eternity before them, now, he had all the time in the world to make toys.

Max climbed the steps to Amelia's front door to find her waiting just inside it to open it to him. She seemed very excited to see him and pulled him into her arms for a brief kiss and swift hug.

"I'm so happy for you to meet my parents at last. My Dad says he has something to speak about with you so be forewarned." she said.

"Got a clue what its about?" he asked.

"I believe it is about the wedding. We haven't really planned our honeymoon, you know, so I think it may have something to do with that. But here they come now, so, we will find out pronto, yes?"

Her parents were walking up the path from the guest house nestled under the huge oak tree in Abigail's side yard. They meandered along the pathway, through the herb garden where the wedding would take place and then up around the bushes to come up the front steps as Max had just done.

"Good morning, people." said her father.

Good morning greetings sounded throughout the friends, joined by Claudia and Josie as they joined the group, yawning. All proceeded into the house where Abigail had already set up breakfast dishes of fruit, breads, cheeses and jams. Hot tea and coffee, along with juice would wash it all down. Thus began a day full of lovely surprises.

Chapter Seventeen

Thomas and Max had decided to take a long walk, which Thomas declared would take them well into the afternoon so to have a lunch packed for them. Though only a little bit anxious, Abigail packed them some sweet things to eat along with more fruits and sent them on their way. Max could take care of himself and she had the wedding plans to contend with. Waving good-bye, she turned and went back in to get to work.

Max lead the way towards the inter-coastal waterway that wound its way down to the shoreline where the land met ocean. The water way twisted quite a bit so that it touched both his property and the back half acre of Abigail's, too. Following it now, they walked along its edge for over an hour until they finally came to where it expanded out into a very broad river and that, into the ocean. Having reached the river, they turned south to walk its edge until they could hear the ocean's roar. When they finally reached the mouth of the river, Thomas turned and pointed back towards a small key island in the river. Max was familiar with the tiny island but had never gone there as it had been claimed already by the time he was given land choices. He felt very fortunate that he had been blessed with having land along the waterway as, when the tide was high, he could take his small sailboat out to the ocean.

"That is my island." claimed Thomas.

"Really!" exclaimed Max. "I had no clue. Abigail never told me. Although, by rights, it never came up in our conversations. Wow, you did good, didn't you?"

Grinning, Thomas nodded his head. "Yes, Cora and I did good. We built our home there, high in its five oak trees but only stayed there a few months before the assignments to work with dolphins came along. Cora and I talked about it and we decided to offer it to you two for your honeymoon, if you want."

"Are you serious? I feel sure Abigail will love it and I know I will."

"That is part of our wedding present to you. The other part I will show you now."

With that, Thomas pulled out a whistle from his breast pocket and blew three sharp toots. He waited a few minutes, then blew three more sharp toots. Just twenty-five feet out into the river, four dolphins leaped out of the water, synchronized in their leaps. Max grabbed his future father-in-law's sleeve and gasped at the unexpected visitors to the river.

Thomas then blew one long sound followed by two short toots and the dolphins arose in the water to stand on their tails, chirping the whole time. Thomas pulled off his shirt and long pants and, in his trunks, waded out into the river. Max was too excited to question the action. He became thoroughly enthralled when Thomas held his hand straight up over his head and one by one, the dolphins took turns leaping up to touch their nose to his hand. Then he dove into the water and disappeared. Max held his breath. It was taking a while but he knew the human lung capacity was much greater in this new world than before. Suddenly, a dolphin rose up out of the water with a grinning Thomas holding on to its dorsal fin. With obvious hand signals from Thomas, the dolphin was directed to make turns on demand just as you would riding a horse. A few more examples of what dolphin and man could do together in this new world and Thomas released the dolphin. All four dolphins followed him as he swam back towards the shoreline. Walking up the beach, he turned and bowed to the dolphins. They, in turn, clicked and nodded their heads. A brief clap of his hands and a side gesture to depart and the dolphins were headed back to the ocean.

"That was so amazing! Has Abigail seen this? I can't believe she hasn't told me about this yet." exclaimed Max. He could only stare in amazement at the man who, though was at least thirty years his senior, didn't look a day older thanks to the reinstalled anti-aging DNA cell restored to mankind.

"Oh, she doesn't know yet, either. Remember, our work started in the Mediterranean after we moved. This would be a gift to her to have my dolphin friends here hooked to a small pontoon to pull you both out to the island. I wanted you to see them perform so that you would not be in fear of an upset or accidental dunking. Clark and Ella are weaving garlands of their glow-in-the-dark plants to put on the raft as well as the dolphins to light the way and let us all see you as you go on your honeymoon. The trick is to get Abigail to agree to an evening wedding."

"She will agree once she knows, though." reasoned Max.

"Well, we thought...wondered if perhaps it should be a surprise for her. What say you on that?" asked Thomas. Max pondered on it for a few minutes and then grinned.

"I think it is going to be the most beautiful wedding and lovely surprise anyone could receive. I just hope we are correct to do it this way. She doesn't have a fear of water or anything. I've heard her speak of times when young where she would go sailing with you. It will be good. I'm sure of it." he declared.

"Good. Now lets eat the lunch she packed us and head home. Cora is going to begin suggesting a later time frame to get Abigail inclined towards early evening. We shall see, when we get back." He clapped his hand on the shoulder of Max, who stood about two inches taller than his future father-in-law.

They needn't have worried as Cora had worked on things from her end by exclaiming over the delights of Abigail's garden while walking with her father last evening. She had wondered aloud if it were possible to have it closer towards the evening so that guests could appreciate the lovely garden at both day and night times. Abigail didn't even blink an eye and agreed with her one hundred percent. Cora kept her smile to herself at how easy this was turning out.

When the men returned, there was a lively discussion all

around about the wedding plans in the evening and how lovely it would all be for the guests. They planned the banquet table to look similar to the ones found on the cruise ships of the old world, covered with seasonal fruit and veggies. Garlands of flowers would be used on the garden arch where it resided between two gardenia bushes in bloom.

The cake would be three-tiered and decorated with fresh, dainty pansies, rose buds and leaves. When they first had to develop their own cooking recipes from natural sources instead of the convenient stores filled with manufactured goods, the libraries left behind provided all the information needed to create baking powder from the wine making process. The crystals that formed in the wine barrels were potassium bitartrate and when you added the mined soda and extracted corn starch to milled wheat flour, milk, eggs and honey, you got a lovely cake.

So much had been destroyed at Armageddon and yet what was left behind was more than enough for the millions remaining. Once all those who had died were resurrected, there would be somewhere around nine billion residents on the earth. It would then be filled and reproduction would cease until further information was revealed by Jehovah God. But for now, a wedding was in the making and a new couple would begin their lives.

Chapter Eighteen

The wedding was beautiful. It was of a period theme in honor of the resurrected former King David, who had arranged their meeting. Abigail wore a sleeveless, cream colored dress with an empire waist, floor length and gold buckles at the gathered straps. Deep purple flowers graced her hair and bouquet thanks to Aunt Violet's contribution to the wedding. Max wore a simple tunic of linen with a draped purple cloth, swagged under one arm, then up over one shoulder with gold buckles that matched Abigail's.

Max watched as Abigail had walked down the lane on her father's arm, he could see the resemblance between them. She had her mother's glorious hair of spun gold and vivid blue eyes but she had her father's full lips and wide, innocent eyes. If so blessed, she would make beautiful children that he would love more than life itself. His love for her showed in his gaze as she walked towards him.

Abigail saw waiting for her, the man who had captivated her heart those many months ago. His tall, tanned body was somehow both lanky yet muscular. His smile with its dimples could drive her mad with longing. She felt stirrings within her being that made her feel both secure in love and free with a soaring spirit. She knew he loved her as deeply and strongly as she loved him. Their love would produce beautiful babies, she thought. Then when she saw that look in his eye that told her he was thinking of their honeymoon, she blushed all the way down to her toes and lowered her eyes. When she reached his side, her father kissed her cheek and went to sit by his own bride of over one hundred twenty five years.

Max's fingers slid under her chin to raise it so their eyes could meet. Their love for each other shined forth with such intensity that it was nearly palpable to everyone there. After the brief talk given by the elder they had asked to do their services, they shared their vows. Max took her hand in his and spoke his heart.

"Not since God split the first Adam has anyone found a love like mine. The treasure I have found in you is worth more than any treasure found in earth. How deeply my love is for you would rival the core of the earth. Now that we are one, let us go forth this day more whole than we've ever been and more loved than seems possible. You are bone of my bone, flesh of my flesh and I love you more with every breath I take." A light chuckle had arose at his joke of splitting the Adam but subsided quickly when his heartfelt message was revealed.

"My sweet Maxwell, how long have I prayed for your arrival. You are my gift from God, which I will treasure eternally. Our love means so much more because we include our God. I love you. I give my heart and soul to this union." she spoke quietly.

180

The elder marrying them finalized the ceremony by presenting them to their guests as the new Mr. and Mrs. Winters. The couple turned to look at their guests. In the moments before they walked towards their reception area, they noted their friends and family there. His father, Maxwell sat next to his daughter, Angie with her husband Eric. They sat behind his mother, Ella with her new husband, Clark, the resurrected Brian and new baby girl. On Abigail's side sat her parents, Thomas and Cora, Her Aunt Gail with husband Jim, her uncle Joe with his wife, Violet. Her friends, Claudia and Josie were her attendants while David and Jonathan attended Max. Her friend, Helen, from the old Atlanta area had arrived just prior to the ceremony and would stay in Abigail's bedroom for the night prior to her return home in the morning. The remaining guests were members of their congregations and neighbors.

The celebration went on for two hours while the sun slowly sank in the western sky. A brilliant burst of red light filled the sky as the new couple danced their last dance of the evening. As the song ended, the group parted ways for them to make their way, hand in hand to the dock. There, four dolphins were waiting in the water beside a beautifully decorated pontoon boat. It was only about five by ten feet and sported two cushioned seats. Four hoops resembling small hula hoops were attached on the outside four corners of the boat which the dolphins would use to pull them. It was decorated with the glow-in-the-dark ferns and orchids, gifts of

Ella and Clark. As they sat down on the seats, guests threw rose petals over them.

Thomas gave the signal to the dolphins to go to the island's dock and off the couple went to begin their new life together. Everyone kept waving till they were far down the waterway and all that could be seen was the glow of the plants surrounding the newly weds.

They arrived gently at the dock of the island and Max took Abigail's hand to help her onto the dock. Tying the boat to the dock, he gave the signal that would release the dolphins like Thomas showed him. All four dolphins stood on their tales and chirped their happiness to be free to go, then took off back the way they came.

Holding hands they made their way down the path to the base of the tree house where their lovely honeymoon would take place. Plants, similar to the ferns that had lighted their way here on the boat, now lighted the way through the well landscaped yard that surrounded the huge live oak tree. There were eight huge tree branches spreading out from the lower twenty feet of the tree. These were the base for the most fascinating tree house they had ever seen. They levitated to the east balcony to explore it. Two large rooms were balanced on either side of the trunk's fifteen foot circumference, with covered enclosed halls for access. Both rooms were decorated with the old art nouveau style, which blended well with God's creation. The huge vines that were twisted in intricate designs were art itself. They twisted and turned to form a kind of screen or room divider. Highly polished, it gleamed in a beautiful way that only wood could achieve. The two rooms were a bedroom and kitchen-living area. Both rooms had balconies off them and upon reflection, it became obvious one faced west and one east for sun watching.

The bedroom had sheers gracing the windows, which billowed out with the gentle breeze wafting through the window. Scented candles were placed throughout the room waiting to be lit upon occupancy. Combined with the floral scent of the arrangements someone thoughtfully placed throughout the home, it became part of a wonderful memory for the couple so much in love.

The next two weeks were spent exploring the island where monkeys played, lemurs swung among the branches and beautiful birds and butterflies flitted about. They spent a great deal of time exploring the beach on the east side of the island. It had a great many sea shells and pieces of driftwood, which they saved as souvenirs of their time spent there. They say on the balcony to watch the sun rise and sat on the other one to watch it set. They glowed with the sun and their love.

As much as they enjoyed their time on the island, it would soon be time to go back to reality and their work. They decided to take a walk down to the beach one last time. Max seemed hesitant to say anything at first but then courage swelled up inside him and he broached a subject that they had thus far side stepped. Children.

"Abigail, we need to discuss something we had lightly mentioned in the past and it is something we really need to talk about before we go home."

"Go home. What a lovely sound. Well, what is it we need to discuss?" she asked.

"Children. And not if, but when. We've made some sketchy plans for the immediate future but that is just our first year. What are your wishes as far as having children are concerned?" he asked.

"Well, of course this is something I have pondered over since the day we met." she smiled, shrugging her shoulders at her questioning look. "All women do that, you know. But, we both have very fulfilling roles to play in the general scheme of things for at least the next year. Do you think we should plan now or do you want to wait and see what happens as things unfold in this new world of ours?"

"Hmm. That is a good point. We don't know what our future will be by then. They hand out new assignments at the beginning of each year and since ours is nearly finished after only five months, we are free to accept new ones as a couple. I guess it would depend on what we volunteer for as a couple. Well, that brings us to a new situation and back to the subject of children. If we want children sooner than later, we shouldn't volunteer for certain tasks, should we?" he mused.

"This is true and a very good point. I guess we have a lot more to discuss, don't we?'

"Yes, and here is the perfect spot to do so. Come, sit with me here on this huge driftwood. Our favorite spot of the whole island." He pulled her towards the gnarled old cypress trunk that had fallen over in some storm but been washed clean of abrasives by years of salt water rushing over it. They situated themselves upon it to where she would lean back against his broad chest. He leaned slightly forward to rest his hands on his knees for support. He loved feeling her back against his chest, now that she was his in matrimony.

"Abigail, let us discuss what we would both like to do for our God and each other, shall we?" he started.

"Yes, we need to do this now, don't we? So, let me say first off that, I would love to have children with you. But, I think we owe it to them for us to get to know each other better, to plan each one and plan how to teach them." she turned her head slightly to look up at him. "Don't you?"

"Most definitely! So, let us discuss what we want to volunteer for now as a couple. What had you planned?"

"Oh, had I not told you that my task as life coach was nearly over? Now that we have reached that certain stage in resurrections, the ones returning now are mostly of the Native Indians. Pocahontas was resurrected last month and they've trained her to take my place here. So, you see, I'm free to pick and

185

choose according to what we want to do. But what about you and your music you and the band write for Jehovah God?" she asked him.

"That was just for fun, my dear. That was not an assignment. I make instruments and toys, which I can continue to do as it does not interfere with our plans, whatever they may turn out to be."

"Oh, of course. I had forgotten the woodworking you do. We have been too busy, haven't we?"

"Busy and distracted." he laughed. "But what lovely distractions to have. So, I've been approached by someone wondering if I would be interested in starting training classes locally for dolphins. What do you think? Could you see us doing something like that together?"

She turned excitedly in his arms.

"Are you serious? Train them like my parents? Oh, my darling, I would love it!" she exclaimed. She jumped up and spun around to pace the sand in front of him. She was so excited that her words were coming out all jumbled and nearly incoherent.

Laughing, Max stood up to grab her hands hoping it would slow down her words, too. All it did was slow her down minimally. He had to place a kiss on her lips to slow down the ideas, plans and excitement that had burst forth from her lips.

"Well, now. That is a job I will enjoy in this new life role of mine. Slowing down your excitement." he joked.

186

"Oh, it will be a full time job, I assure you." she grinned back at him. "But since that could lead to unplanned children, let us walk off the excitement and sit in the comfort of the tree house to sketch out what we can do. Okay? We will need to see about setting up the construction of the training building and classrooms for both people and dolphins. Mother shared many of her interesting stories about setting up their school. Oh, I can't wait."

"Well, you don't have to." he stated simply.

"What do you mean I don't have to?"

"Your father had been working with the idea with some elders prior to his trip here and the success of his dolphins traveling the distance across the ocean to be here was all the proof needed to assure the success of a local school. He will leave two of his life mated dolphins in this area to assist in training new students and dolphins. If you had agreed, and I had hoped you would, we would set off for training with your parents for six months this year while the school is being built along the coastal bay area."

Abigail merely grinned and pulled him into the house. She didn't stop at the living room area like he thought they would do. She quickly by-passed it to head for the bedroom. Grinning to himself, Max decided he definitely loved married life.

Chapter Nineteen

When they arrived, via the dolphin pair's pontoon boat, they were greeted by her uncle, Joe. He had known there would be many questions about the marina and its dolphin school if Max's grinning face was anything to go by. He didn't realize, however, the enthusiastic response they got from Abigail. She was truly a force to be reckoned with when it came to the details of the marina, the training program and assignments of duties. Max dealt with the construction side of the project while the engineering department worked with what adjustments they needed to make from the Mediterranean design they had to go on.

So many buildings and equipment had been left undamaged by Armageddon which made some things easier in this new world. But all things decay with time, so many resurrected scientists were constantly finding new ways to add years to newly constructed buildings. New forms of plastic, which would be consistent with using the oil preserves correctly while not damaging the ecology of the planet were under investigation more and more. The brilliant minds thought to be lost to death had been brought back, reeducated and given new tasks, to their delight. Since the human brain was beginning to function at its full one hundred percent capacity, many new inventions were coming along at a rapid pace.

The space program, turned over to private businesses in the

old world, was shelved for the first seventy five years. Then, one day, at one of their conventions, it was revealed that the space program would be opened for review. Space exploration, thought to be impossible in the old world due to the short life span of humans, was now being considered as a strong probability in the future. Planning a type of space ark to house transplanting animals, plant life and humans was something already in the works for the approval of the governing body once they got the approval from Jehovah. It probably would not take place in this thousand year rule by Jesus, however. Perhaps, once the final test when Satan was released was passed, there would be space travel and new planet colonizations.

In the meantime, there were too many projects in the works and still many thousands of years of people to be resurrected. For the next two hundred years, there would be people returning from the dead and needing to be trained and skilled. That is where Max and Abigail planned to be of help. They wanted to expand the possibilities of trained dolphins, plus whales. The mammals of the ocean were of good use to mankind and the projects of cleaning the ocean floors of debris. Plus, it was just plain fun.

Max and Abigail had spent their first week in their home together setting things up for sharing with each other. Living with someone was very much different than living alone and both knew there would be major adjustments. In view of the fact that both were mature adults made it so much easier. They fell into a routine that worked for them both and much joy was experienced as they settled in.

Max's home was a sprawling one that had been left behind as a spoil of victory at Armageddon. It was over twenty-five hundred square feet with six bedrooms and bathrooms for each. He had to install a septic system as the sewer lines of the city were no longer functioning at the present time. Since he was the only one living there when he first took occupancy, it was of little consequence. The future growth of his family would be dealt with in whatever way would be needed. The interior was very open, light and airy with modern furniture that never seemed to wear out. One of the benefits shared, no doubt, with the Israelites who roam the wilderness forty years and their clothes nor shoes wore out. What a loving God he had, he often thought. The garden was one to rival the great knot gardens found in old England. A kitchen herb garden was just outside the back screened porch while an orchard was found just beyond it. A three car garage had been converted to his studio where he built the instruments he loved to hand out at the festivals. The toys were a side joy, with which he liked to surprise the newest young ones. As he looked around the shop upon his return with his new bride the thought occurred to him that he would one day make toys for his own children.

"Abigail...Abigail!" he yelled out as he went running into the back door.

"I'm still unpacking in the bedroom." he heard her answer.

He rushed into the room which was off to the right of the kitchen.

"I just thought of something else we have to consider.!" he exclaimed, breathlessly.

Abigail went to him and put her arms around his waist.

"My darling, whatever it is, it must be something to make you breathless like this. What's on your mind?"

"How many children do you want? I don't know how many children you want. We joked about it on our honeymoon but we need to be serious."

"Oh, is that all? I want how many you want."

"But, my dear, don't forget that I was there when Angie was born and I know why it is called labor pains. How much of that would you want to go through? How much would I allow you to go through?"

"Max, what ever are you referring to? You know we won't experience that kind of pain in this system. No more pain, remember?"

Max nearly collapsed under the relief of the strain he had unnecessarily caused himself.

"Oh, that's right. What an idiot I can be when it comes to your comfort. What was I thinking?"

"I would say you were thinking how much you love me and how much you would want to spare me." she smiled.

"I'm still not certain about our future but it sure looks brighter since you came into my life. It is certainly going in a different direction than I had ever hoped it would, so I'm thrilled with it now. I do love you to distraction, you know."

"And I love you too." she sighed as she pulled him closer to hug him. They kissed.

"Twelve." he said.

"Mmm. Twelve. Twelve what?"

"Children. I want twelve children." He called out after letting her go and walking towards the kitchen once more.

He laughed when he heard the choking sounds coming from where she resumed her unpacking.

Chapter Twenty

Six months later

Max and Abigail had just returned from five months spent training with her parents on the beautiful island just off the coast of what used to be Rome. They were thoroughly trained and efficient in the craft of training dolphins, whales and people. What was lacking in their training classes that hadn't been covered was new and therefore they could participate in the creation of new training for whatever came along. The cooperation between mankind and animals was so intensified since the great battle that amazing progress was made towards using the animals in whatever capacity they would be good for. Elephants, camels, horses and other like animals were used in construction work, hauling things, carrying passengers, etc. Dogs, wolves, bears and others like they were often used to carry supplies, packages or mail and pulling small children's carts. Birds were also used to carry messages or small packages. It was quite normal to see a large breed dog with two side baskets in which a woman with twins would have her children. The animals were totally subject to man and living in perfect peace and harmony just as the Bible had foretold it to be.

As they pulled the horses to a stop in front of their home, Claudia came out their front door to greet them. She had volunteered to house sit for them and payment, though none was required, was half the crops during the time of her stay. She had a basket of peaches in her arms as she came down the flight of six steps to warn them that there was a body of elders waiting for them in their living room and that she would wait on the porch until they were finished with them to give them her full report during their absence.

Max turned to Abigail.

"I wonder if they think I have my report ready. I've only just returned and haven't had time. It can't be that. Claudia, did they say just me or Abigail and me?" he asked.

"Oh, both. They looked quite pleased about something so I wouldn't fret." she replied.

"Well, I was doing quite well till you said they wanted to see me, too." Abigail laughed softly. "Let's solve the mystery by going on in, shall we?

"I'm game if you are." he grinned. They walked in to their living room.

The room had six men seated, sipping a cool drink that Claudia must have served them. All stood upon their arrival into the room.

"My brothers, to what do I owe this pleasure?" Several started talking at once until one man called for silence and began his own explanation.

"Hello, my name is Albert Craig and this is Arly Muller. We were sent down to represent the Governing Body in a very exciting project we are to offer you and Mrs. Winters here. The rest of the brothers here you know from your own congregation, I'm sure." Max nodded and shook all their hands as did Abigail.

"Since you were not part of any committee that is involved in this project, you will have to be filled in about it all, but later. Here is the crux of the matter. We had known of the lifting of the waters just after Armageddon but we hadn't given the matter much thought as to the effect it would have on the polar regions until a few scouts we had sent out to get reports from those regions came back with the knowledge that both polar regions are devoid of human inhabitants. This does not follow in with Jehovah's plan for the entire earth to be inhabited and we were hoping that you would consider being one couple of the sixty couples from assorted countries to go and establish yourselves there. We know it is asking a lot for you to leave your families but since you have eternity before you, you have lots of time to visit. I digress, of course. What we were wanting from these couples are skills useful for promoting good growth and education. You both come highly skilled and completely trained. It is amazing what you have learned about dolphins in the past six months so it is something desirable for you to be among those sent. But, please understand that we will be here two more days to give talks in the area and give you time for consideration and any questions.

But this will all be mute if you are of the decision to not have children. We are looking for couples with the desire to propagate. Is this something you have considered as yet in this new marriage of yours?" he asked.

"Yes, my brother, we do plan on having children. The matter of how many is still up in the air." he grinned as he turned to Abigail. She blushed.

"Excellent, then. We two shall be off to our lodgings while your local elders discuss things with you more. We are staying at the Right Foot Inn while here. I still can't figure out that one. Something about a hokey pokey song. Anyway, you have two days to discuss it and give us your answer. I know it isn't much time, but we need to move on this and if your answer is 'no', then we need to find your replacement. Have a good day and I hope to see you at our talks this weekend." he said as they turned to go out to their maglevs.

They all turned to each other and began to discuss the whole thing very excitedly. Claudia was invited back in as they felt she would give some female insight into the matter and be support for Abigail. They took a quick break while Max and Abigail brought in their luggage and fixed a quick snack for their guests. There were a great many pros and fewer cons. The discussion went off in many directions and had to be brought back into focus several times. Suddenly Max brought up something that they were all overlooking. Their home and what should be done with it. Claudia suddenly broke out with a cry. They turned to her.

"Oh, please, if you would consider this, I have lived here

196

for the last six months and everyday I wake up wishing it were filled with guests to talk to. If you would consider allowing me to open it up as a bed and breakfast, I think it would absolutely fill the bill. It is so huge and empty. I know you wanted to fill it with children but now with this new option you seem to be seriously considering, it would be just perfect for the community and for me."

Max turned to Abigail and they whispered to each other for a few minutes. After some head shaking and head nodding, they turned to her.

"We think this would be a perfect solution with one stipulation." said Max.

"Of course, whatever you want."

"You must promise to not name it the Left Foot Inn." he grinned. The whole group laughed and laid out the plans for their response to the visiting brothers.

Later that night, after everyone was gone except Claudia, they went to their bedroom to ready themselves for bed. There would probably be little sleep for them, the excitement of this challenge so new in their minds.

"Abigail, do you fully realize the importance yet magnitude this challenge is going to be for us?" he asked his wife.

"It certainly presents itself with challenges never before undertaken with the exception of the era where 'go west young man' was prevalent. What is on your mind?" she asked him.

"Not sure if there is anything there specifically or just me wanting you to share your feelings about this new direction we seem to be headed in. How do you feel about this?"

"I feel great but I cheated a little bit. I saw something I know will be shared with us upon acceptance, but it was an accident. I hope you know me well enough to know I wouldn't deliberately snoop." she stated emphatically.

"Of course, I know that. What is it, my dearest?"

"Well, when I put the glasses of wine down for our visitors, the paper laying on top of the Bible they carried was exposed out from the end of the folder. It said; Prepping for Space Exploration." she claimed.

Max's mouth dropped open.

"Do you think they are considering us for that eventuality?" he floundered.

"I think that it is a strong possibility, don't you?"

"Well, I guess so, if you saw that. Was there anything else you saw?"

"No, that was it. I know you think I'm crazy but the thought of going to the polar regions had no appeal to me until I saw that note sticking out. I realize it is a big risk but I think it is also the most exciting adventure we will ever be on. I would love to be the new Adam and Eve but doing it right this time. Wouldn't you?"

"Only since you would be my Eve. But Honey, you realize

this would not take place for another seven or eight hundred years, right?"

"Yes, I know. By that time we will have grown to perfection. But, what better way to prepare for that grand adventure than spending it with you on a brand new island ripe with new adventures, new animals we've never worked with and new plant life to discover. It would be the greatest adventure anyone's had in a long, long time."

"Yes, the great Arctic adventure."

The End

Author's Note

I have really enjoyed doing the Biblical research on this project. There are so many questions answered in the Bible. My hope is that this book gave you some insights into what the future holds. Although I did take some creative license, for the most part, all is possible.

Jehovah is a very loving God and I did ask for his guidance in writing this. He would not be able to help me with my grammar so, for those errors, I apologize.

Please rest assured that the resurrection hope is found in the Bible. The hope of living forever with eternal youth is also found there. That animals will be tame is found there. Please avail yourselves of the website listed below. Even the potential, for those children who died in the womb to be resurrected, is found there.

May this book be some source of comfort to you all. May it bring you some joy as it has brought me in the writing of it.

Gay Miller

Reference work done at ▰▰▰▰▰

27961076R00115

Made in the USA
Charleston, SC
28 March 2014